The Seventh Perfection

ALSO BY DANIEL POLANSKY

The Builders
A City Dreaming

THE EMPTY THRONE
Those Above
Those Below

LOW TOWN
Low Town
Tomorrow, the Killing
She Who Waits

the Seventh Perfection

DANIEL POLANSKY

A TOM DOHERTY ASSOCIATES BOOK
NEW YORK

THE SEVENTH PERFECTION

Edited by Carl Engle-Laird

A Tordotcom Book
Published by Tom Doherty Associates
120 Broadway
New York, NY 10271

www.tor.com

Tor® is a registered trademark of
Macmillan Publishing Group, LLC.

ISBN 978-1-250-76757-8 (ebook)
ISBN 978-1-250-76756-1 (trade paperback)

First Edition: September 2020

For Evie; may you get everything your brother does and a little more besides.

DAY 1

(1)

Unknown

3:23 PM

Chilled melon, mistress? The perfect remedy for the afternoon heat! Picked fresh from my orchard and drizzled with honey. Three kel, normally, but in honor of the holiday, I will give it to you for two.

By the thing that made you, why would you wish to see him? Yes, I know where he lives, but I will do you a favor in keeping silent. Not even Ba'l Melqart knows the hour of our passing, but surely none of us will remain forever above the ground. You would do better to sit in the sun and eat my melons than waste the rest of the day listening to the puffed-up rantings of an old man. The past is the past. Go digging in a graveyard, you're sure to find a corpse.

Will you not try a melon? Two kel is nothing for the pleasure it will give your tongue, and it might go some way toward loosening my own.

~

Forgive me, Amanuensis, I did not—I did not see your brand. Forgive me. Take your second right and follow the alley upslope. His house hangs over the hill like a torn thumbnail. You will not miss it.

Of course, take it and be welcome.

No, no charge. Call it penance for my rudeness, in trying to charge for what ought to have been free. And it will give you something to do during the hours to come. I told no lies on that account. Nutesh is a man who loves the sound of his voice more than bees love roses, more than rats love carrion, more than Amata loved Kiri.

It is nothing. May the God King's eyes watch over you.

(2)

Nutesh

3:37 PM

Yes? Yes, I am he.

Come in, please come in! May I get you anything? Tea? I have a bottle of . . . no? Excuse the mess, I was re-cataloging my collection of pre-Ascension medals. The Anathema's forces—there were few enough honors given out amongst we revolutionaries. Though they were earned! They were earned and earned twice over!

Thank you! I think I do myself no undue honor in say-ing that, as regards the Rising, there is no finer collec-tion of artifacts anywhere in the city, or at least outside of the Spire. Twenty-five years I have been assembling them, digging through stoop sales and side bazaars, keep-ing my eyes out for anything which might keep the mem-ory of those times alive. I had almost given up hope that anyone would recognize . . . but no matter. You are here now. And with the Jubilee only three days away, what better time for a proper reckoning?

Where shall we start? Ah! Here is something special—protest posters, fliers for discussion groups and meetings, all from the old Academy! That one there—with the skyline redesigned as a cage—was drawn by the pen of Laqip himself! We would paste them around the city, or leave them scattered in cafés and parks, but I always made sure to keep one for myself. I was always a bit ashamed of it; it seemed to be taking from the cause. But even back then I knew that we were on the cusp of something extraordinary, something which posterity was owed a piece of, the just inheritance of future generations!

Let us see, what else might be of interest to you? All of these ratchets are from before the Ascent. Their blades are steel, not hard carbon, but the edges remain as sharp as ever. Do you see that one in the center? With argent and purple trim? A collector ought hold no more favorites than a father, but that was the sidearm of Amata herself! I know it sounds like a barker's pitch, but I can state it as a point of certainty. Many were the evenings I saw it on her hip! And it is said she wielded it with great distinction in the battle for the Spire, though I admit I was not there to see her do so.

We met at the Academy, in my poetry seminar that first year. I was far too shy to speak, though this was not a problem for Amata! Tomorrow, on her feast day, you will see many an old man like myself outside of the Cathedral, wet-eyed at her memory. So many were lost in those days, but I think never was there one more justly mourned than Amata. But it was as she would have wished—with her life's blood she ushered in our age, and her memory resides still with Ba'l Melqart, blessed be His name.

No doubt you know that Amata founded the student committee for resistance, her and Laqip. Anyone who was there will tell you that she was the animating force. She organized the students into cadres, she walked at the head of the vanguard during the Sanguinary March, she held the placards when they were bathed in red.

Alas, no. An intestinal complaint, would you believe the luck! One bad bit of street meat and I spent three days retching on the floor. Often I think back on that misfortune, and what I missed. To have been at that crux of history, the hub on which the great wheel turned! Well, we each have our role to play, as Ba'l Melqart tells us. All are valued, from the lowest to the high.

If you seek firsthand experience of the March, you might do well to visit Seluku. He was among Amata's closest companions, and a great aid to the revolution, once upon a time. He owns a club off the Lower Heights, near the Academy. If you do go to see him, you will be . . . polite, yes? If ever a man has suffered, it is Seluku. The things that were done to him . . .

Well, thank Ba'l Melqart that you were born into the era of His benevolence.

The lockets on the far wall? Remembrances, they were called. It was the fashion in the days before the Ascent for lovers to have them made for one another. When opened they present a simulacrum of the subject. The images have faded over the years, but you can still make out rough outlines. Sometimes at night I take one off the wall and wonder after the person who appears—if they are alive or dead, if they have grown fat or withered away. If the person they gave themselves to was faithful or treacherous, if they married and had children, if they loved those children, if they knew regret. I suppose most of them did not lead very happy lives, or they would not have sold away pieces of themselves. They were quite expensive at the time, though these days you can pick one up for a few copper across the Grand Bazaar. Less, if you haggle.

You have one yourself! A fellow antiquarian. But then you would have to be, given the nature of your enterprise. Is there a nobler purpose than to preserve the wisdom of past generations for those to come? Within the boundaries of Ba'l Melqart's laws, it goes without saying. May His light shine in the darkness.

Let me take a look. Do you see this emblem on the

back? It's from the old Academy—why, this might very well have been given by some old acquaintance of mine, some old friend!

Of course, I would be happy to look at the image itself, though I cannot imagine that I would be able to recognize it. We do not all have your eidetic gifts, and if the simulacrum has faded, my memory has rotted twice as swift.

~

No, I'm afraid I've never seen her before. Really, she could be anyone. Twenty-five years is a long time, and there were so many who died during the Rising. I'm afraid Seluku will be of no help to you in this matter. Yes, I am certain. Abundantly certain.

Did I say the Heights? If you say I said it, then I must have—but thinking now, I am not sure how I could have stated it with such confidence. It has been many years since I have visited the Lower Heights. Most likely Seluku has passed over or retired.

It was an honor, Amanuensis. You are welcome and twice welcome. Blessings of Ba'l Melqart upon you, in this, the holiest of seasons.

(3)

Street Preacher

4:43 PM

Ungrateful children! False and treasonous, vicious and undeserving!

You pass by in your ignorance, in your foolishness! You see my rags and you think me mad, but all are naked in the sight of Ba'l Melqart! He takes no measure of your silk and brocade, He cares naught for your diadems and sterling. Your wealth will not avail you on the day of judgment. Samite will not hide your crimes, nor gold deflect your sin; He will read your history on the folds of your heart, and in the strands of your hair, in your eyes and on your skin!

He knows you, thankless children! He has heard the lies you tell each other, the lies you tell yourselves. He has seen the things you keep hidden, the things bound deep, around your heart and your spine, the things which you do not yourself know are false. But He knows! He knows!

Obey His servants with light hearts and smiling faces. Obey the High Chapel, the blessed Patriarch, and his hierophants. Pray that they be merciless in rooting out the apostates and the blasphemers among us, whether they reside in the Enclosure or the towers of Silver Terrace, in our homes or in our very beds!

This week of all weeks, let His companions serve you as examples! Remember Laqip, clever and bold, who turned his talents to the Rising and the new God. Remember Amata, who was kind to all things which deserved it, who loved our lord with a faith noble and true. Remember Kiri most of all, Kiri who overthrew the Anathema, Kiri who became Ba'l Melqart.

Instead you dance and you frolic, you boast and you brag, you gossip and you blaspheme! In the evenings the clubs and the music houses and the alleys of the Scarlet Way are full, but in the mornings the pews of the High Chapel sit empty. You make a god of your pleasure, you see no good beyond your loins. You strain and you kick against the laws He has put before you. You do not see that His dictates are for you own ease, are for your good, would bring you joy, and above joy, peace. If only you would see, if only you would see!

But you will not see. You will not see until it is too late!

(4)

Seluku

He's very good, is he not, Amanuensis? One of the best drummers we have ever had at the Fourth Perfection. No, no trick, I assure you, or at least no more than the usual artifice of the blind. Gaszi is very good, and there are many who come here and find their feet tapping along to his happy rhythm. But they do so imperfectly, they do so gracelessly—they can't replicate his syncopations, they lack his feel for the pocket. I think there are only six or eight other drummers in the city who could perform such a task, and I know all of them. When they come in, they yell, "Seluku, bring me a drink" and "Seluku, let me hold a few mina till payday." Drummers are the most profligate members of a reprobate species—not a scientific fact, only a judgment born of long observation.

Thank you. It is all that's left to me these days, to appreciate if not to create. It is enough. We accept what we cannot change. I was known to tap the snare on occasion, though my specialty was the long harp. I was thought to have had some talent in my youth, not that I imagine my meager abilities would have been anything against your own. Speaking of which, perhaps you might be interested in sitting in on the next set? It would be a great honor for the Fourth Perfection to host one who has actually perfected that skill.

In that case; what can I do for one so high in Ba'l Melqart's service?

I haven't thought of Nutesh in years. No doubt you found him buried in tarnished metal and faded drapery? A mother hen atop an antique egg? You have done an old man a kindness in making him feel important enough to warrant a conversation. Did he tell you of his days as a revolutionary, hand in hand with blessed Amata? He knew her, that much is true. Everyone who attended the Academy in those days knew her, and a great many others as well. She was—perhaps famous is not quite the right word. The city is vast, and I do not imagine any but a small proportion ever heard her name in the years before the Ascent. But anyone involved in the movement knew her.

The question is, did she know him? And there, I am afraid, the answer is a bit muddled. No doubt she smiled at him at some point, and perhaps even shared a laugh, or offered him a sweet word. She was very kind; more than anything, she was kind. But beyond that?

Well, who can say? I am aware that unerring recollection is the final perfection mastered on the White Isle, but for the rest of us memory is a slippery thing. What I ate for breakfast yesterday is more a matter of conjecture than of fact—and as to the distant events of my youth? A story, altered and added to with every telling, the rough edges evened out. Who is to say that mine is any more accurate than your would-be historian's? He meant well, at least.

No, I will not say anything else ill of him. This was before the Ascent anyway, and the God King's amnesty certainly covers his crimes. If Nutesh yelled louder than he fought, if he never found himself at the front, facing the servants of the Anathema . . . as I said, there is no glory in condemning the pretensions of an old man.

Besides, not everyone can have an injury to boast of. I received mine before the Sanguinary March, when we still had some hope that the crimes and iniquities of the regime were the result of the Anathema's ignorance and the corruption of her minions. We were . . . we were still very naive. Our meetings were illegal, but then, everything was illegal in those days; you hardly paid attention. The only organizations sanctioned by the Academy were study and prayer groups, and even those were ribbed through with informers. It was a running joke that there were two in every class; you could tell because they were the ones taking notes.

Amata and Laqip started it, a few of us meeting at cheap coffee shops before curfew, talking with that mad passion of youth, certain that the problems of the day were as simple to diagnose as to cure, and that we were destined to play surgeon. Forgive me, that was an old man speaking, and old men have no more love of youth than a starveling for a glutton. I suppose every generation wishes to upend the works of those that came before, to put their own distinct mark upon the earth. The young see things in such stark divisions and imagine—cannot help but imagine—that their own time is uniquely terrible, that they are but a step or two from apocalypse.

But that does not mean that they are always wrong. The city had grown to rot. Here along the strip, where the cafés now extend out forever, and pretty boys and handsome girls strut hand in hand, there were nothing but boarded-up houses and long lines of begging veterans, flesh burnt and tumescent. In the Trace, where smoke parlors and boutiques now bleed into the Grand Bazaar, a shantytown stretched for miles, tents and scraps of cloth for the lucky ones, the dust or mud for most. When I was a student I took a room in a house not far from there; I lasted two weeks, and then I moved in with

Laqip, a mat slung on the ground for twice the price but I was happy to pay it. You will find there is none of us can look very long at the depth of human despair. Not that this is much concern for me any longer.

That was a bitter joke. Apologies again.

In time our conversations became meetings, and these meetings outgrew our tiny apartments. We began to gather students outside of our cohort, and people who were not students at all but just come to listen to Amata and Laqip, to dream some of this shared dream. We took to holding our discussions at the house of one of our wealthier members. That was what we called them, *discussions,* as if doing so would hide the fact that we were discussing the rot that had infected the city, and how to clean it. At first it was a game as much as anything else; I can admit that, I who paid for playing. We thought ourselves *very* clever, stealthy as mice and brave as eagles! When we had a meeting we always made sure to have two exits, and we demanded the most *terrible* oaths of secrecy from everyone who would attend.

A man may swear to a thing and not mean it. And a woman also, though I think less often. Regardless. I am not sure who it was that betrayed us that night. We never found out, or it was decided best not to tell me. Our meeting was stilled by the rap on the door downstairs. We knew that sound, even young and foolish as we were, knew to fear it, the sound and what would come afterward.

Of course, we need no longer fear such things, in this happy age. As everyone knows.

We were all making for the back door when Amata stopped us. If it hadn't been for Amata, none of us would have escaped, they'd have gotten us all in the bag, and then who knows but for the revolution? No Sanguinary March without Amata, and without that afternoon, the wretched heat and the blood in the streets, perhaps Kiri would never have . . .

But that is a pointless sort of speculation. They were at the back door also. I don't know how she knew that, but she did. Nor do I know how she was aware of the hidden staircase that would lead us down to the aqueducts below the city.

Some of us, anyway. The door was hidden behind a heavy bookshelf. At least it seemed heavy to me; I can still remember straining my shoulder against it. By the time they found me I had put the thing back in its recess, and I was sitting on a chair, smoking a cigarette. I have no idea how I lit that cigarette, my hands were shaking so badly, but I managed it, as I managed with the bookshelf. They found the passageway after a few minutes of searching, but those few moments were enough.

Some have called me that. But what does it mean to be

brave? A moment arrives, no time for thought or for consideration, terror thick as syrup in your veins, the rhythm of your heart going faster than Gaszi could ever drum, and you throw yourself left or you throw yourself right. It is an easy thing to be courageous when you do not know what is coming, and no one who has not been through it can really imagine. When the magistrate declared against me, when they set me down in the chair, when I saw the red tip, felt the heat, heard the sizzle—in that moment I would have killed everyone I had ever known to save myself, I would have betrayed Amata and Laqip and my own mother, I would have done anything they asked of me. Can we call that courage? Can we really?

The hands were not part of my punishment, not officially. A gift from the guards, powdered sugar atop the bun. Perhaps they had heard I was a musician. Perhaps they had not. I am inclined to think the latter. Cruelty is like the drums or the great harp; some of us have some peculiar talent, but even for mediocrities, practice makes perfect.

I wasn't much use for the cause after that, except as a martyr, and we had plenty of those. I saw Amata once or twice more, but then came the Sanguinary March, where she met Kiri, and then went underground, and so on and so on. That part of the story is common knowledge—or at least I have nothing particular to add to it.

Here I am rambling, and after all that I complained of Nutesh doing the same! I suppose that old men are as one in such matters. Regardless—was there something specific you wished of me?

He had that much right, at least. Yes, the remembrances; they were popular when I was a youth, though I haven't seen any for a long time. Another weak attempt at humor. In any event, you will have already gathered how little use I can be in tracking down the woman in your hologram.

Not at all. I am sorry I couldn't be of more help. May His blessing rest firmly on your shoulders.

(5)

Gemeti

Manet? Manet! I knew it was you! I could tell from a block away, by how smoothly you slid through the crowd. Of course, it's easier when half the men go statue-still when they see you. Which perfection is that again, remind me?

A joke, a joke! But you must sit. I'm meeting a friend for a hubble-bubble, but that's not for ages, and I like you far more than I like him. I haven't seen you forever, not since Pirhum's birthday. Do tell him I said something naughty about him— not too naughty, Manet, I save that honor for you!

But you must! As if I could hope to finish the whole thing on my own. That's a good girl, don't stint. This is proper spring sour, broken out fresh. They only make six barrels, in honor of the Jubilee, and frankly I'm shocked they've lasted this long. Have a taste, you'll be surprised as well. See? Was I wrong?

What are you doing in this corner of the city? You've come early if you think to see anything interesting. The Lower Heights don't get going until well after nightfall, though I suspect it will be even later with most of the city outside the High Chapel, waiting for tonight's pyrotechnics. No, I can see in your eyes it's not that. If not personal, then it must be business? Are you off on some special mission for the God King? Investigating injustice, stirring up secrets? Or is he simply curious to know which public house in the Heights serves the best beer? Let's see, coming east you'd have passed Mistress's Gaze, the Summer Blossom—they have the most gorgeous servers, though the food barely passes muster—and then there's that old jukejoint with the hideous décor, the something Perfection, what is it again, can you remind me?

Oh, I *jest*, Manet. What's gotten you in such a foul mood? Is Pirhum not taking care of his end? Too busy at the hospital, I'm sure he says, but that's hardly an excuse for failing to—

I see.

I'm so sorry, really. Please forgive me. I hadn't heard. When did . . . but no, let's not talk about it. It must have been recently or I'd have already heard. But let's not mention it, please. Another glass of beer, so that I have something to fill my mouth with besides my foot. Yes, yes, you too, otherwise I'll spend the rest of the evening sure that I've offended you terribly, and I know you wouldn't want that.

Oh, fine, fine, I muddle along. Apart from the boy and the hubble-bubble, little enough. There is Wardum, but he's nothing more than an occasional distraction. Good for a throw, but as soon as he starts talking I have to pretend I've fallen asleep. Men are all little children; either they can't keep a civil tongue in their heads for the half hour required to prove themselves gentlemen, or they're timid as squirrels. I swear, you got the last good one.

I've done it again, haven't I? I might as well salt the wound proper. What happened?

Yes, we have to say those things, don't we? But I have seen the way Pirhum looked at you; you don't need to pretend the decision was mutual. Then again, there are different sorts of choices. Some people leap straight into cold water, and some wade in an inch at a time, shivering all the while. And there are some who need to be pushed.

It just struck me—this is your first Jubilee since leaving the White Isle! Oh, you lucky, lucky thing! I'm green with envy, positively emerald! To see the whole spectacle for the first time, the parades and the illuminations, the whole city promenading about in their finest. Let me top you off, there's a good girl. Why not? Why not? If ever there was a night for joy, it's tonight, and if ever there was a place, it's here. But then, that's true every night and everywhere, so far as I'm concerned. What's the point of despair? Find yourself a man and forget about Pirhum—as much as you're capable, I suppose. What a strange thing it must be to hold every past moment forever, perfect, as if you've just experienced it!

At least you shouldn't have any trouble with the first part. Even a breed would scarce fail to find an escort during the Jubilee, and with the kink in your hair and the way you hold your eyes as if you might eat the person you're staring at—yes, that look right there! Perhaps wrap up your brand first, though. I suspect men find it a bit intimidating to chat up a girl who can remember every word they say.

If you're really desperate you could head to augur alley for a palm reading. We used to do it back in school, trade a few mina for the name of your next love or anything else you'd care to ask. It worked well enough the one time I went. She predicted I'd go to the winter formal with Ellu, though she omitted that he'd vomit cheap wine all over my white dress.

Come now, Manet, it's just the two of us girls. What are you doing all the way down here in the Heights? You know I'm so curious I could just cut my wrists on the table! No? Nothing? Not even if I promised to sew my lips shut after? You're a cruel thing, a cruel thing. Pirhum is lucky to be rid of you!

Oh please, four glasses isn't enough for you to find a sense of humor? How about five, then? Probably just as well; I'd like to be faintly sober before I head to the pipe.

What a happy surprise this was! Let's do something again soon; you know I'm free all the rest of the Jubilee. You still remember my address? Forgive me, what a foolish question.

(6)

Mother Anu

9:35 PM

Welcome, welcome, and once more welcome; take a seat and tell Mother Anu your cares. Money? A concern for all who labor on this side of the divide. Love? Beauty is no safeguard against heartbreak, is it, my child? I can help, whatever you need. Not for free, of course, but for a reasonable sum, more than reasonable, meager even, when measured against what I offer. I am a proper augur, as it says above the door, versed in all thirty-seven methods of prognostication. Palmistry is quickest, though least reliable. The bones take only a few minutes longer but are more accurate, in matters of business especially. If it's a question of love I would have you hold a candle as still as possible for a full minute, then scatter the wax against a bit of folding paper. But if you have the time and the inclination, I suggest the tea leaves. It is the most expensive service that I offer—two mina, as mandated by the guild. No reputable augur would charge any less.

Excellent. Just a moment then, I'll set a kettle. Black or green? It makes no difference in the reading. Green it is then, better for the stomach. You'd best put your shawl above the door! Wet clothes lead to a bad cold; you can have that for free.

~

Amanuensis . . . this is quite an honor, to play host to one of Baʻl Melqart's slaves. I had not expected . . . but I suppose there is no reason why a recorder would be any less interested in her future than the rest of us.

That noise will be the tea. One moment.

You are . . . very blunt. Is this a demand of your order? It is true that there are many who claim foreknowledge, and some who are foolish enough to believe them. But I am fully credentialed, a member in good standing of the Sodality of Vaticinators. My dues are in order, my papers signed and sealed. My trade is a legal and honorable one, my prices set out by the common agreement of the guild. Of course I am not always right in my predictions; doctors are not always right with their diagnoses, but we still have hospitals. The future is not stone. The future is a trail of ivy or a budding rose—a skilled gardener might predict which way it will grow, suggest ways to improve its flowering, but they can do nothing if you choose to tear the plant out by the roots, or if some great flood comes and washes your farm away. I am right more of the time than I would like, does that satisfy you?

Now, you are halfway through your tea and have not yet said what it is you wish to discuss, nor have you offered your payment. Two mina. The tea is complimentary.

~

Take back your silver. I have no idea who is in your keepsake and would not tell you if I did. How strange, for I have always understood that the last and highest perfection was that of memory, and yet it seems that you have forgotten everything I've so far said. Do I call your craft into question? Do I dispute with you between a high C and a low? Do I quibble with your rhythm, or suggest that your recollection is anything but infallible? You could as well do me the same courtesy. I read the *future*, girl. That is my craft, that is my calling, that is the work Ba'l Melqart allows me. You ask about the *past*, and the past is a slippery thing, best left alone.

Amanuensis or no, you are drunk and talking foolishness. Do you know what the most difficult part of my job is? It is not the work itself; I have always had an easy knack for teasing out the strands. It is knowing when to stay silent, when to lie outright. They do not come to me to know what will happen to them. Most already know. You are a carpenter today? You will be one tomorrow. Your husband drinks and is cruel to you? Men are brutal and rarely mend their ways. Your daughter coughs scarlet in late autumn? She will be dead before the spring. Life continues without purpose or meaning, then ends abruptly.

But they do not come to Mother Anu for hard truth. They come to hear that everything will turn out well, that they are not fat or foolish, that happiness awaits round the next bend if only they can hold out that long.

I have no idea who is in your keepsake. I cannot give you that answer, and neither could any of my colleagues along the row, though some of the less honest might tell you otherwise.

But then, not everyone is affiliated with the guilds. There are powers older than Ba'l Melqart, there are things that even he does not know, or at least of which his servants remain ignorant. You are very brave to threaten a woman with the heavy hand of the High Chapel. If you were a bit braver, I might know someone who can tell you who is in your locket.

That will be a full talent. The guild does not set the price for secrets, and I charge you extra because you can afford it. And because you are rude, and rude needlessly.

The coin first.

Head north, until the shops are replaced with cheap taverns. Then east, until these too end and you come to empty houses and houses in which no one ought to live. When you find yourself nearing the great bridge, search carefully for an old track leading downward. At the bottom of that ravine, beneath the bridge where it is always night, there is a shack. In that shack there is someone who can answer any question you care to put to them.

I do not know her name. She has forgotten it or traded it or tossed it away. I cannot tell you her price either. It will be more than the two mina for the tea, that much I can say.

If you are wise you will not go tonight. The cliffs would be dangerous if the ground was flat and level, understand? If you are wise you will wait to sober up. If you are wise you will not go at all; but then, wisdom is not among your seven perfections, is it?

Leave your cup where it is. I do not need to read your leaves to know your future. You head toward a ledge at a dead sprint.

Sweetness and the Crone

10:15 PM

You're right, Sweetness, she does look like a rat! Staring at some morsel from cover and making up her mind whether to snatch it. Or a cockroach! Or a cockroach! No, a rat. Yours was better.

Will she cower there all night? It makes no difference to us. For us it is morning and the cock has just crowed. We have naught to do but wobble on our wobbler and puff out our puff, perhaps natter down and look at the spray. Has she seen the black waves roll against the black beach? All black beneath the bridge, in the shade. Does she know there are different colors of black? You are the one who taught us that, Sweetness. Yes, you did. Yes, you did.

Ooooh, she comes! See her skitter, Sweetness, see her run! She is a brave little rat! Or is she hungry? Hard to tell with a rat. Hard to tell with a girl. She looks sleek; a girl's hunger is not a rat's hunger. Sit, sit, little rat.

Or do not sit, it is all the same to us. Is she hungry? The soup bubbles. There are men on the shore who leave us little presents—stonefish head and squid tail. For the knife, you see, for the bowl. Do not fear, there is plenty.

As she likes. As she likes.

A very pretty little rat to be coming all the way down to the Shade. How did you find us? Who told you of us? Did she come from Silver Terrace? Could she see the Spire, from where she came? I think so too; she has the smell of the towers all over her. But how did she learn about us? They don't talk about us in the high city, do they, Sweetness? They may think about us, they may even visit us, but they don't talk about us. Do you remember the one who came with last month's moon, wearing that heavy black cloak and the hundred-talent dress beneath? Took her diamonds off but not her powders. She wanted to know how to keep her man, and I'll spit in the soup right now if he wasn't at least a potentate. They all know about my Sweetness, yes, they do.

Hee-haw! Hee-haw! In the alley? With their scarves? With their crystals? With their cozies and their porcelain? *Hee-haw! Hee-haw!* Funny little things. Silly little things! Like the children who play on the beach, wetting their toes and running from the waves as they crash. Not us. Not me. Swam past the breakers, I did. Drank a belly's worth of brine. Will die drowned, will lie at the bottom to be nibbled by the fishes, to rest with Sweetness and others that live there.

She is sure she does not want any soup? Flavored with cuttlefish ink, and other things. We make it very tasty, we do. We both agree on that.

If she does not want soup then what does she want? She wants an answer? Ask the question, then, ask the question! *Hee-haw! Hee-haw!* Do you see her? She expected more! She thinks that we are like those girls in the alley, with their dice and their cards! She expects a show! Do not be so rude, Sweetness, she does not know any better. But there is no show to be found in the Shade; only Sweetness, and the things Sweetness knows.

Well, then; let us see it.

~

Never met her.

So impatient! I agree, Sweetness, she does not deserve anything, not when she cannot wait a moment for an old woman to speak. Too kind, but lover's eyes tell only lies! Skin like broken glass, and more gum than teeth! At least I've kept my figure. But then, I only eat what goes in the bowl.

I said that *I* did not know. Sweetness might. Sweetness

knows many things, but he does not tell them all, do you, Sweetness? And a good thing for us! They come for truth, but they do not want it, do they, Sweetness? No, they do not.

What would she give for an answer? I gave the second finger down to the knuckle, and the left eye and its stem, and the flap of skin which was between my legs, gave and not taken gently. Sweetness remembers, Sweetness has not forgotten.

But we were not talking about me, Sweetness, we were talking about her. What would she give? Would she give the very tip of her tongue, to make her sweet voice stutter? Would she give the nub of her nipple, and rob some future babe of suck? Would she bring us something for the bowl? So many sad things in this city, so many things that would be better in the bowl. But still they struggle. All things struggle, don't they, Sweetness?

The rat is scared again! Perhaps the rat is not so brave as we thought she was, Sweetness, so brave or so hungry! What did she think, that knowledge was worth nothing? That she could get it for free?

She should go away. Yes, I know we said we would help her, Sweetness, but what can we do if she is not willing to pay, Sweetness? They are not our rules, Sweetness, we did not make them and we cannot change them. If you wish a thing you must give a thing. And she is not a brave rat after all, she is just a foolish, fat little girl. She should go back to wherever she was before she came here. Because she does not want to know! Not really, not enough.

What does it matter to her anyway? Who cares about the face in the locket? I do not care and neither does Sweetness. And she does not care very much either, if she will not even offer us a little something for the bowl. Just a cut! Just a snippet!

∿

Hee-haw! Hee-haw! We are surprised, aren't we, Sweetness! Even an old woman can be surprised! Old but not so ancient as that! She should not worry, a quick nip and then into the bowl. I will burn it after, so it does not rot.

∿

Hee-haw! Hee-haw! A hard little rat, a hard little rat! Didn't scream at the chop, did she, Sweetness! Into the bowl, into the bowl. The knife is the easy part, though; the knife is not near so bad as the cauter.

∿

There now, all done. Just a little thing, barely notice unless you play the long harp. A tough little rat you are, a brave little rat. No, Sweetness, be fair now, they all scream at the burn. We take back what we said—she is a hungry thing, she wants to be fed. I think she is as hungry a thing as we have ever seen.

Well! A bargain struck, a bargain honored. Sweetness says that if she wishes to find what she is looking for, she should head down to the spray and follow the current until the moon is straight above her, then turn inland until the stench becomes too high to stand. Where the city dumps the things that they do not want or think to forget, she will find the wreck of an old trolley with something very nasty written on it. She should sleep there, or try to sleep, until she is woken by the sun. Scuttling along the road the next morning she will see a man wearing blue, and she should follow him until he has gone where he is going.

Yes, that is what she should do.

Hee-haw! Hee-haw! She wants more than an *answer*! She wants the why of it! We do not know the why, even Sweetness does not know the why! Even that sad fool atop the Spire does not know the why! If there is a why. But we think there probably isn't, we think it just is.

She can stay if she wishes, she does not need to leave. We like a bit of company. Not that it gets lonely, never lonely, not with Sweetness here. We have such fun, the two of us! She is sure she will not stay a bit? Rock some on the wobbler? Have a bit of the soup she has made?

Hee-haw! Hee-haw! Goodbye, little rat! Starved for answers, but she will have her fill before long! *Hee-haw! Hee-haw! Hee-haw!*

(8)

The Half

11:47 PM

Mine! Mine! Not yours, mine! From the rusted trolley to the edge of the ducts, bought and paid for. Mine in perpetuity, mine till I rot, mine forever and ever and ever! He got his kingdom but I got mine, sovereign and indissoluble! My minions may be carapaced and hexapedal, but they are loyal! Are they not loyal? An obeisance with an antenna is an obeisance nonetheless!

One ought never approach a monarch empty-handed. Don't you know anything? Would you approach *him* that way? No, you would not! And are we any worse than him? Are we?

~

Excuse us! Even the highest potentate, even the most magisterial of magnificates can make mistakes. Even a god has no claim to wisdom! Remember that I said that. Will you remember? Someone really ought to.

In any case, your offering satisfies! The button is very fine, but the thread is simply marvelous. What was I saying?

There were three of us that climbed the tower. They say there was only one, but there were three. Now there are only two. One and a half. Can you call the one a one now? I do not think you can. I think you must call that one another number. I do not know what number that is. Infinity is not a number. Infinity is not a number! And anyway, infinity can become zero; that is not so difficult a thing at all. One can make infinity a zero, if that one is brave enough.

Half was brave once. Once half was very brave. Once half knew no fear, once half sang and everyone sang along because they knew that half was not afraid. Once half was one full one. And what a one half was! Once half was the cleverest thing you could find! Half could sing a song or paint a picture! Half could doodle! Half could hum!

Why does the moon look like that? Do you ever wonder? Wander? Do you ever either? Is it fair that the moon looks like that, and will look like that after we are gone? No, it does not seem fair to me either.

But you must excuse me, you are welcome and more than welcome to my hospitality. The button was very fine, as I said, and also the thread. The thread was . . . well, I fear I have lost it. In any event! Sleep comfortable! I offer you sanctuary within my demesne, protection from the pawed and the clawed and the moonlight which will shine when you are gone.

DAY 2

(9)

Minder of the House of the Full Peach

11:55 AM

If you seek employment, you will find the matron on the second floor—though you might take a bath first. You look like you've spent the night rolling in filth. For that matter, you should have someone attend to that finger. Though perhaps that will appeal to some of the clientele. In any case, it is the matron's concern; I'm here only to maintain the safety of the staff and guests.

Few enough this time of day, the one in blue was our first. And fewer still make trouble, but my ratchet is self-cleaning, and my components remain in working order. Mostly the sight of them is enough to turn away the poor and the moon-eyed. There was a man who came by last night who claimed that Tabni looked just like an old lover. He wished to give her a bouquet of frangipani—but the house does not take frangipani, only coin. He sat with me on the stoop and spoke of a son he has not seen in many years. I did not mind listening to him; I am told it is how the girls spend most of their time. Still, I hope he will leave us be; the matron says if he returns, I will have to hurt him.

In any case; if you wish to see the matron, one of the girls inside can guide you. Otherwise, be off.

~

Forgive my rudeness, Amanuensis—I intended no disrespect. I had not . . . I did not . . . Forgive me. I am willing and thrice-willing to assist you, though I don't imagine I know anything of interest to Ba'l Melqart and his slaves.

Yes, it's all backed up internally. I cannot claim your gift of memory, but my condition allows for a standard of recollection that no normal human could match. My banks will not rot for a very long time yet, though I record less; light and sound only. It has been forty-nine years since I tasted anything, and though I am aware of pressure it is not the same as touch. There are times when I think I can recall the smell of the ocean on the sand, the rotting fish and the sea salt, the close-wet reek of my family, my own distinct scent. . . .

But I haven't offered you a proper greeting. Welcome to the House of the Full Peach, or at least to its doors. We are number 343 in the official licensing, copies of which the matron would be happy to provide, the originals of which are kept safe in the High Chapel. We host thirteen registered consorts and two former members of the staff who act as caretakers. And the matron, as I said. And myself.

No, not at the moment. We have a doctor who visits twice monthly. Precautions are taken. Not perfect, but then what is? On those occasions when the aegis slips, most of the girls choose to terminate. But that is their choice, and not one forced by the house. We have had children in the past.

You may call me the Minder, or anything else etiquette allows. I have not used a name for a long time, since I was first fettered at . . . seven, or perhaps eight. Since entering my new form forty-nine years, six months, thirteen days, six hours, thirty-nine minutes, and twenty-seven seconds have passed, but I cannot speak with certainty of the time before. There was little to tell of it. We lived on the outermost shores of Seaside. I am told that estates of great wealth now run along the seawall, even dripping into the breakwaters, but in my day there was nothing of the kind. The richest among us lived in shacks of driftwood and tarpaulin. My family was not among the richest. The only thing in the world of which we had a surplus was children. A common story.

There were always brokers at the market, mustachioed

men with booming voices. "Serve the city, help your kin," the predictable pitch. They gave me some tests—simple math, a cup and ball to check my coordination—and decided on my model. I was excited. Protection seemed better than maintaining the aqueducts or working the high steel. They gave me a small pamphlet regarding the form I would take. I could not read the words, but there were pictures, and in the weeks that led up to the procedure I would stare at them by the little light of our vapor-lamp, trace my finger along the lines of my jets, and the twin ratchets. A few more years and it would have been pinup girls, though we are fettered before we reach that point. I am not sure why, but youth is a requirement.

As for the transition itself, there isn't much I can tell you. There are no words to describe the External, or if there are I never learned them. It is said they know nothing of time but everything of everything else, that they will answer any question you ask but never in the way you wish, that they can shift and shuttle about the minds of men. That last, at least, is true. One instant, I was flesh and bone and sinew, ten fingers, eyes of . . . no, I cannot anymore remember the color. In the next, I was as you see me. My services were purchased in perpetuity by the house. By a different matron, in fact; I transferred ownership with the bill of sale.

We are a long way from Seaside, though my family

made the journey a few times. Three times. Once they all came, or nearly, there were so many it was hard to ever be sure. The next it was just my mother and sister. Then my mother alone. I asked her not to come again; it was easier for everyone. Most fettered prefer to have no contact with anyone from their previous existence.

But surely none of this can be of any interest to you, and you will forgive me for speaking so long. If you would tell me of the specific nature of your inquiry, I could be of greater assistance.

A holographic projector, I gather? And as for the image . . .

~

Who are you? What is it you want? There are things which are best not discussed, not by anyone, not by your kind or by mine. However pitiful my existence, I would not have it end.

No. No. Forgive me. I would never imagine going against Ba'l Melqart, blessed be His name. Blessed be His name. I will tell you whatever I know.

Yes, I recognize her. She called herself Rose, but I never supposed that was her real name. Our records of that time were destroyed in a fire years ago, and our matron wouldn't know either. It was a different matron, as I said. I'm the only one left who knew Rose.

She arrived in the early afternoon. She looked . . . ragged. Too thin, and dirty, and tired. But still she was beautiful beneath that, very beautiful, and our house was not so well-established as to be turning away talent, even if it needed a buffing. I sent her in to see the matron, knowing well that she would be accepted, and then I waited for the ones that would follow.

Many different girls have passed through these doors. Some come because they do not see any difference in the life they are living and the life they would live here, save that in the House they are compensated for things elsewhere taken. Some come because they put no high value on the services they offer, some few because they so enjoy offering them. But some come with the look Rose had, of being chased. Fathers, lovers, former managers: it does not matter. I am here to meet them.

This was in the bad days, just after the Ascent, when the city was in an uproar and none knew what to expect. Four of them arrived that evening, dressed as thugs though that was not what they were. I am not sure, but not that. Twenty-four years I had watched the house by then, you may believe I could tell a footpad from a counterfeit. Their clothes were cheap but not worn, and their flesh was smooth. There is no bravo worth his salt who does not have a ratchet scar. Even the very skilled ones allow themselves to be marked as proof of their badness.

Also, one of them carried a beamer, which even in the days before Ba'l Melqart's peace was very rare. Only the military or perhaps the very wealthiest of the syndicates could provide such a weapon. No manager rich enough to carry one would bother to hunt down a single employee.

No, not thugs, though they dressed as them and spoke the same. Big words, meant to cover up their fears. They are all afraid when they see me, even the very brave ones. It has grown tiring, listening to the same sorts of chatter for fifty years. I explained to them that the girls inside were property of the house, as I was property of the house, and threats against us would not be tolerated.

Three of them had ratchets. Those did not concern me. There are not enough men and not enough ratchets in the world to concern me. But the one with the beamer . . . the fettered are not invincible. A blast from one of those to certain portions of my frame would have been enough to obliterate me. The leader—or in any event the one speaking, although the loudest man is rarely the one making the decisions—raised his weapon and repeated his demands.

Shall I tell you what it is that makes me so dangerous? This structure which I inhabit, it is not the same thing as a body. Steel and silicone are not flesh, not sinew. For your kind, thought must precede movement, and violence is a peculiar state, one you must work yourself into. For me it is as easy as turning a switch; a 0 become a 1. Or a 1 become a 0. I struck with the plasma jet on my shoulder. It has been a long time since any of my kind have come equipped with them—the replacement batteries are terribly expensive, and only good for a few shots. But they are very good for those few shots. The one with the beamer the houseboy cleaned up with a mop. The two closest received only the spillover, and screamed for a long time before dying. I decided I could not allow the last to run. A few cuts with my hand ratchets—replacement cells for the jets are expensive, as I said, and I saw no need to burden the matron with the cost.

That was the end of it. The end of that part of it. Except for the beamer, it was not particularly noteworthy. I could tell a similar story about any number of other girls, though it is true that mostly their pursuers have enough sense to leave before I am forced to perform those acts for which I was constructed. Her arrival was not special.

But Rose was.

I am not allowed in the house proper, unless there is some trouble which requires my presence. The official reason is that I make the patrons uncomfortable, which is true, but it is also true that I make the girls nervous. The fettered are discomfiting to you who remain free. Even you, Amanuensis, you stand at a distance, and when my gears whirl you blanch and move back a step. No, do not try and dispute it—it does not offend me. It is the natural reaction of flesh, and anyway I have had a long time to grow used to it.

But Rose did not . . . she was not afraid of me. In the mornings or on slow nights she would bring out a stool and sit beside me and we would talk, and sometimes play chess together. I was better than her, but then I have little else to do but sit outside and play chess, and so my success was more a matter of practice than ability. And anyway, I was not much better—347 games to 254 as white, 320 games to 234 as black. If she was in a good mood—which was not very often, especially not after . . . not in the later days of her service—she would recite poetry. Once she told me she had known the poet, but she did not tell me their name.

I never knew what brought her to the house. I did not ask her. It is a peculiarity of your profession, this constant need to question. It is one which would win you few friends, did you not labor in service of the God King. She was only here for a few years. She was a good earner, Rose, as kind as she was beautiful, and she had many regulars happy to pay for the pleasure of her company, not even always of going to her room, just sitting on the veranda and chatting with her, as she would sometimes chat with me. And she saved what she made; she did not spend it on drink or puff. When she left she had enough money to buy a little shop in the Reaches, and an apartment above it.

Or so I heard. I have not seen Rose in twelve years, six months, thirteen days, and some eleven hours.

~

. . . a child?

I cannot remember.

Did I say that? Then I was lying. If my banks are superior to the memory of an unfettered, still they are imperfect. There are gaps in my memory, there are holes, and that is one of them. An error in my processing—you may take it up with the External.

I have nothing further to say. You have used enough of my time.

Will you? Will you really? After this conversation will you march up to the High Chapel and swear out a complaint against me? You will do no such thing, and you know that you will not, and I know that you will not. Like a bravo, despite your brand—loud words and foolish threats.

Wait—wait. There is one more thing that I will tell

you. Rose was very smart; she was as clever a woman as I have ever met, and I have met many. She had a very good reason for coming here, and if she didn't choose to tell me what it was, that does not lessen my certainty on the matter. You might consider why a woman of such gifts would choose to hide in a house such as ours and go by a name which was not her own. You might wonder who sent the men I killed that first day.

You might wonder many things. Were I you, I would do so in silence.

(10)

Qem

A kel, mistress? With a kel I could buy some fried bread and meat from Tommen who sells them on the quay. It is pork today, and pork is my favorite, when I can get a kel, which is not very often.

Thank you kindly.

Qem is my name. I didn't used to think it was too short, and I would tell strangers that my name was Ahati-waqrat, which I thought was much better. But I have come to like Qem; it sounds hard and plain, like the thud of a cudgel. A man should not be ashamed of what he is. Anyway, Qem, yes, and a pleasure to meet you also.

Auntie Rose, you mean? I *can* take you to her. *Will* I? I might. I am a busy young man, I have much to do today. Time is money, you know. You knew that? Still. A guide will cost you a mina.

The kel was only a kindness, the mina pays for my service. You will not find her otherwise, believe me. The roads in the Reach are like a cracked pane of glass; there is no sense in how they run. And not all the inhabitants are so friendly as I am. Not that you need fear so long as I'm around; this is my neighborhood, from the lapping sea to the top of the knoll.

Very good, then. Money first. Not that I do not trust you, mistress, only that here in the Reach . . .

Honest silver! You won't regret it.

I can tell you a story about her as we walk, if you wish? No extra charge! Though if at the end you think it worth something, I wouldn't throw it in your face.

You know about Auntie Rose's store? Twine and needle, hard candy and molasses, coffee, cheap clothes, that sort of thing. A hard business, not much money to be made even for a sharp operator, and Auntie Rose . . . well, my mother must have died owing Rose seven mina, and she never asked for it.

But that was long after, and the story I am telling you is about back when Aunt Rose first came to the neighborhood. She was not from the Reach, or Cliffside, or anywhere else around here, and when she spoke, which was not often, she sounded like soft cloth or like she was singing a hymn. We were all confused by her, even Enusat who used to run the neighborhood. Now Libluth runs the neighborhood, though there isn't much difference between them, except Enusat was fat and Libluth is thin.

Anyway, it was Enusat who I saw come into Rose's shop one afternoon while I was in the back corner, looking at some of her candy I had no money to buy.

—Good afternoon, Auntie.—

Enusat said that. Rose was at the counter, as she was most afternoons, knitting, as she was most afternoons.

—Did you think about what I said?—

Aunt Rose continued knitting.

—It's a good deal.—

Still Aunt Rose did not say anything. From now on I won't say anything when she doesn't say anything, I just won't say anything.

—You won't be bothered, Auntie, my boys are solid. They walk in, they nod, they get the package from the back, they nod, they leave. Like they weren't ever here. My boys are solid.—

I had stopped looking at the candy by then and was peering through a rack of cheap coats.

—Maybe you're worried about the Chapel? No reason. You'll have seen by now they don't come down here much. And those that do are reasonable men, solid. Solid like my boys. Maybe it is the money? The money is fair. More than you must make in a month selling twine. And you can still sell your twine, Auntie. Nothing will change for you. My boys will come in, they will leave, and in between it will be like they were never there. It is a fair price, especially because I do not need to pay it.—

Enusat kept picking things up and putting them down, like an old woman about to haggle. I was careful not to say anything, or even to breathe.

—They tell stories about you.—

This was the first thing Aunt Rose had said; I noticed that and so did Enusat. He came and sat on a stool across from her.

—What do they say?—

—That you have done hard things. That you are a hard man.—

—Do you believe them?—

Aunt Rose set something on the counter.

—Do you?—

Enusat snarled and puffed up his chest.

—You had best put that away, Auntie, before you hurt yourself.—

Have you noticed that people will often laugh when they are afraid? That was not how Auntie Rose laughed then. It was a real laugh, like when one of us kids tried to leave her shop without paying for something.

Enusat had nothing to say to that laugh. After a moment he got up and walked out, and then Aunt Rose told me I could come out from behind the coats, and she put away her pistol and gave me some rock candy.

It was a little one-shot pipe; I am not sure how she got it. There was a lot about Aunt Rose I never knew.

A little while after that Libluth took over the neighborhood. Perhaps he had heard what had happened with Aunt Rose. Perhaps he had not. Enusat was a mean bastard—excuse my language, but he was—and I do not remember anyone crying the morning his body was found broken at the bottom of the cliffs.

She was a special woman, Rose; I miss her often. Here we are.

No, mistress, I did not lie. I told you that for a mina I would take you to her, and here she is, below that tuft of posies. It's a nice spot, don't you think? We wanted to give her a headstone, but we didn't have the coin. Those flowers are mine. I mean they are hers, but I planted them there, and I water them during the dry season.

The fever, three years come spring. She did not suffer long. We brought her soup and bread, and we even took up a collection to bring in a physick, a proper one, from the Lower Heights. He gave it back to us after he had taken a look at her. Some of it, at least. Grasping bastard.

We closed her shop after; there was no one to take it over. Rose had no children. Or she never spoke of any, and no one ever came to visit her. If I was hers, I would have come to visit her all the time.

What was left of her stock we sold to Nuratum, her competitor, on his shelves the next day and twice what Auntie Rose had charged for them. Her clothes we sold to the rag man, her books to a merchant in the Old Town. His name ... let me think ... his name was Puzu. The whole library he bought, nine mina, a very good price, I think. We split it between us—me and some of the other boys. I used my cut to buy a cycle, but the battery died last summer, and I cannot afford to replace it.

It is a good place, don't you think? It would be better if we did not have to die, but if we must, and I suppose we must, then at least we should lie beneath green grass, and yellow posies, not so far from the sea.

Are you sure you can find your way? It might be best for me to walk you back down to the main road. It is a tricky path, as you have seen, and not everyone in the neighborhood is so friendly as Qem.

As you wish. It is your two mina. Speaking of which, do you suppose that my service is not worth some little bit extra? It was a very good story, after all.

Thank you kindly, mistress. I will leave you to it, then. Blessings of the God King on Amata's day.

(11)

Puzu

Welcome to Abiditan and Sons—an honor to play host to one of the God King's slaves. If you would be so kind as to close the door after you, Amata's parade has been passing by since high sun, and while I have nothing but esteem for Ba'l Melqart's love, I've grown weary of the cacophony of her followers.

Thank you. Welcome again, as I said. Feel free to peruse the stock. I had a full set of Nasha just last week, though alas, that has already been purchased. Hard to keep them in stock, though who can say why? A pale, pitiful imitation of Samum, himself an overripe epigone of blessed Laqip. We have just gotten in a selection of Zaza's latest, if you like that sort of thing—though I see by your face you don't. A woman after my own heart! I would sooner burn them than sell them, but... need makes must, yes? If it weren't for cheap melodrama, I'd be out of business before summer.

Puzu is my name, the eponymous "Son." My father is long dead, and the title alas dated. Still, there is something to be said for tradition. It is a very lovely sign, and after all it is not as if we have ceased to sell books and begun to sell cutlery—the name of a thing is less important than what that thing does.

I sell books. I collect them, I catalog them, I care for them, and in time they leave me. It is a bit like being a father, though my books do not yell and whine and soil themselves. I have a close relationship with all the major printers, carefully cultivated, though most of the stock is secondhand. Less lucrative, but there is something about a used book, is there not? Each one a little bit of history, a piece of the life of a stranger. Sometimes you get lucky and find an inscription: "to Kammani, with love," "to Igmilum, in honor of their first degree." My regular clients keep me in steady supply, three they have already dog-eared for one they have not yet enjoyed. It is a strange sort of pusher who will trade stock for stock. You will see no similar arrangements among the poor devils who beg for puff.

Consignments? Now and again, not as a regular part of my business. Rose? I'm afraid . . . no, it doesn't bring anything to mind. Oh, the children! I had forgotten the woman's name, forgive me. I was skeptical at first,

I thought the books might have been stolen. When I said there is nothing I love so much as a book, you understand that was a bit of hyperbole. Righteousness is to be regarded above any other good, even aesthetic, and I would never dream of straying from Ba'l Melqart's laws.

But anyway, the guard confirmed the children's story, and so I was happy to purchase the lot. I did not know this Rose, but she had fine taste, truly an exceptional eye. There were three works of the poet Etel-pisha, very rare, and a copy of Arammadara's history of the Rising, though as I recall that one was so badly mauled I had to get rid of it for a lonely kel, as if someone had marked it in a rage. There was even, now that I think of it, one of Laqip's first editions. The first editions since the Ascent, that is to say; I have heard that that he had some books released during the last era, but they must have had a very small run, because I never saw one. In any event, they would have all been long expunged. You may rest assured that every book in my shop carries the High Chapel's stamp and has been deemed acceptable by the chief censor.

Yes, I was here for the purge. As I said, Abiditan and Sons has been on this block for more than fifty years. We were fairly compensated. I did not follow them to the incinerators, so I suppose I cannot personally affirm my stock disappeared into its flames. But I have no reason to think otherwise.

A barren place my shop seemed, back then! Thirty titles were released in the first year of the new era, the Holy Tome and some commentaries, biographies of Kiri and his companions, histories of the Rising—not very good ones, not very thorough, nothing like Arammadara's magisterial work, but something at least. Each year the High Chapel has seen fit to release a few more, and by now the shop is nearly as full as it was before the Ascent.

Very nearly.

I would not think to question Ba'l Melqart's wisdom, but you can understand how a man in my position would mourn such a loss. I have heard that to the north of the city, along the endless plains, there are great herds of horned elk. Every third or fifth or seventh year a plague will infect some portion of them, drive them cancerous or mad, taint their meat, and in response a cull will be ordered. The men whose job it is to herd these creatures, to raise and breed them, they are the same men called upon to perform this grim task. I do not imagine they enjoy it, do you? It is one thing to lose a few every year to slaughter, as my library is depleted by sales. But to see all go at once, endless mounds of souring carrion . . .

Still they kill them. As I signed away my stock, every

line, jot, and tittle. As I said, I am not one to question Ba'l Melqart's wisdom.

But we were speaking of the children's consignment. I bought the library in its entirety, tip-to-tail, as it were. Not even a talent! A thing is worth whatever two parties will accept, is that not the case? The boys who brought me this library were smiling at the end of the transaction. And I? I was smiling twice so wide.

I have already mentioned the few I found particularly noteworthy. The rest were mostly poetry, with perhaps a few mysteries tossed in—but then, the true gourmet is one who appreciate variety. What sort of a person sits down over a meal of chicken and laments that it is not beef? And who would wish to live only off beef, anyway? There was nothing in particular about them that I can recall, no notes or bills, not even a particularly memorable inscription, if that is what you mean. Nor, I'm afraid, can I give you any idea of who purchased them. A large sale, or a very expensive one, I might make a note of, but for these small purchases? I do not keep those, I'm sorry to say.

Was there something else you wanted? I have all the time in the world for a slave of the God King, but there are many tasks requiring my oversight. . . .

I imagine you would know more of the White Isle than I. Children who pass the initial tests are taken east, where they undergo training in the seven perfections—rhythm, ear, voice, touch, body, word, and memory. Of a hundred that begin, only half attain the first perfection, and half the second, and so on and so forth. That small fraction who complete their training are entitled to the brand, and return to the city to serve as the God King's memory.

How was that? Full marks?

That would be ... the perfection of word? No, that's the sixth. The fifth would be the perfection of body, then. Complete control over every muscle, from the bicep to the last joint of the hallux. As to what exactly that means, again, you would be better equipped to answer. I confess I am unclear as to what direction you ...

A fascinating point, Amanuensis, though I struggle to grasp its relevance. I have been entirely candid, and thus your preternatural sensitivity toward falsehood, one acquired along with the perfection you mentioned, would not come into play.

Because it is a hot day, and I am an old man. Old men sweat.

I know nothing about that. I have no trade in prescribed books. Never, not once. I have not made a single mina off their sale.

~

Surely, mistress, you would not ... it's nothing, as I said ...

~

Yes, by the Spire! I could not stand to see all of them go to the inferno. Not all of them. But I was not lying, not really! I don't trade them. They are mine and mine alone; I keep them hidden in the back. The rest I could give up, but not these three. I have no children, and my parents died long ago. You asked me was I compensated, as if my stock was iron ore or bales of cotton or tins of jellied mutton. Can you compensate a man for the loss of his family? Can you compensate a man for the loss of his soul?

You would laugh if you saw them. A book of myths from when the Anathema first assumed her position, so yellowed and bent that you can barely read them. A volume of Jana's poetry. Yes, you can buy a new copy, but you cannot buy *my* copy any longer. A new copy would not have been given to me by a dark-haired girl who I knew for one summer and never saw again. The last? *Slough Bear and the Swampmen*. It was the first book I ever owned. My father would sit me on his lap, and he would read a page, and then I would read a page, until one day there were no pages left to read.

What drunkard would have such fondness for his first

bottle of wine, I ask you?

And there you have my full confession, congratulations. Shall I continue? Is the record of my blasphemies insufficient to condemn me before the High Chapel? Fine. I care no more for Ba'l Melqart than I did for the Anathema. They were neither of them anything to me. My life was no different the day before the Ascent than the day after. I awoke—I ate breakfast—I sold my books—I ate dinner—I fell asleep. And far the larger portion of the men and woman who dance and cheer and sing in the streets this morning, you can hear them right now if you listen, far the larger felt the same way.

Now that I have revealed myself, debased myself, now that my head is on the chopping block, what is it you will demand? Money? I have little enough, though you are welcome to the till, and there is a small safe in back. There is nothing in the world that I would prize above my safety . . . or only three things.

But I don't know! If you have such powers as you pretend, then you will see that on my face. I never met the woman, and all of her books are long sold. I have no idea what became of them, I swear! What is it you wish me to tell you?

Why would I have any idea who's in your locket? Wait! If that's what you want. Show it to me.

~

Excuse my laughter, Amanuensis. Yes, I recognize the image. You hardly needed to go through so much trouble. Look out my window and you might see her a dozen and a hundred times, staring from the icons and the placards passing by. It is her day, after all—Amata the benevolent, whose love was the rock upon which Kiri built. Amata who went up the Spire, but did not come back down.

(12)

Nutesh

3:47 PM

Amanuensis? What ... what a pleasant surprise to see you again! Though in fact I was on the way out. The parade is not for another few hours, but I had hoped to go early and find a decent spot to stand. Perhaps we might have this conversation tomorrow?

No, of course. Enter and be welcome.

I ... I can look at it again if you wish, but I can't imagine what good it will do.

As I said—her face means nothing to me. I wish I could be of more help.

~

Perhaps there is some dim resemblance, but simulacrums fade with time, and really I can barely make out more than an outline. The curves of the face, but ... but only barely and still . . . she could be anyone.

And anyway, the icons are hardly . . . as I said, they . . . they do not do her justice.

Go away. Go away and do not return. For your sake as much as mine, leave and do not come back.

I recognized her as soon as you opened the latch. Do you think I could have forgotten her eyes, I who have dreamed of them every night in all the years since? Do you think me a fool? Letting me rant and rant, and then slipping it sidelong out of your pocket, and do I recognize, and have I ever seen? I do not know how you managed to hold on to that locket and I do not care to know. It has no meaning. It is not what it seems.

Because Amata had no children. Three went up the Spire, but only one survived to face the Anathema. Only one, and that one was Kiri, Kiri who became our Ba'l Melqart. This is the truth of the matter, as every schoolchild knows. To speak otherwise is blasphemy, and anyone who would do so an apostate. Amata died. She died saving Kiri, whom she loved, who became Ba'l Melqart, who looks over all of us. They bore no issue—he is Ba'l Melqart, seedless, without heir, the eternal and the singular.

And if it was otherwise—if Amata had lived, and if she had been swelled with child, and if she had delivered that child, then what every schoolboy knows would be a lie, wouldn't it? And who knows what else might be false, if that was false?

I have nothing else to say. Go away, Amanuensis. Go away and never speak of this again. Crush that locket with a stone and throw what is left into the sea. Take a ship to some distant land, to one of the foreign cities.

What? Yes, why not? Take the ratchet; the purple and the argent go well with your color, as they went well with hers. But it will not be enough protection, that I can promise you.

You foolish, foolish girl. You foolish girl.

By the God King, you look so much like her.

(13)

Gemeti

5:37 PM

Manet? What are you doing here? What have you done to yourself?

You look awful, and you smell worse. I'd offer you something to steady your nerves, but I suspect you've had plenty of that already. Sit down—no, not there. That is the *nice* chair, and you seem to have spent the last day rooting in filth. Yes, there. The one with the stains.

But . . . look at your finger! We need to get you to a doctor immediately. . . .

Slow down, slow down. You're not making any sense. You went where? And spoke with whom?

~

Yes, I see the locket. What is the point of it? Amata? A . . . passing resemblance, I suppose. They both have dark hair and dark eyes, like you and I and half the rest of the women in the city. Fine, fine, say it is her? What does that matter? Why should that have worked you into such a state?

~

Manet, I cannot . . . I will not pretend to understand how it must feel to have been taken from your family at so young an age. I can imagine how that would leave . . . scars. But surely you realize that what you're saying is madness. Nonsense. Every orphan girl in the city must have some similar fantasy.

He said that it was Amata. And who is *he*, exactly? A hoarder living in the tenements? And you believed him? Because men *lie*, Manet. Because he liked the idea of having something important on his wall, or because he paid a great deal for it and did not want to feel a fool. Or he lied because he was lying to a beautiful woman, and he thought the more he lied the longer you'd listen. Men lie all the time, to themselves even more than to us.

I paid a visit to Pirhum this morning. Because I was worried about you, obviously! Seeing you now I think I made the right decision. He said that you've been acting irrationally. He said that after the locket arrived you grew . . . obsessed, and that you left the house the other day in a huff, and he hasn't heard from you since.

I am told that the seven perfections come at the expense of... that is to say, it is my understanding that sometimes those blessed to serve as Ba'l Melqart's memory struggle to... that there is a cost to so high a position.

I was simply asking a question. Is it not true that graduates of the White Isles are prone to... confusion? Some occasional instability? Then is it not possible—is it not *possible*—that this fixation you've developed on the locket is the result of your professional hazard? Pirhum seemed to think so, and while I would usually discount the opinion of a jilted lover I'm rapidly coming around to his point of view.

Of course I'm worried. I worry when a friend comes running into my apartment unexpectedly, dressed in the clothes she wore the night before, stinking like an outhouse, her small finger cut to the bone, talking madness and hiding a ratchet in her jacket. Are you looking into a sideline as a bravo? How do you even know how to use one of those?

Oh, perfection of the body, of *course*. If dancing were the same thing as killing, every club girl would be a mass murderer. And who will you wield it upon, dare I ask? Who will be the audience for your new performance?

Better. Better. Just calm down. Here is water. Drink it

first, then go to the bathroom and pour some over your head. No favor, I assure you, or rather one that you do me. You have picked up the unmistakable odor of dog shit since I last saw you. We should throw out what you're wearing.

The locket will keep! The locket will not walk off alone into the city while you're bathing. Take it with you then, whatever you want.

Shower first, then talk. I've some clothes that should fit you, though the pants will be tight around the waist. I'll lay them on my bed, then run out and pick us up something to eat.

Please, Manet, calm down. Take a long shower and see if . . . see if some of these ideas don't simmer away in the steam. I only want to help.

Patriarch Shadrach

6:43 PM

Hello, Manet. Please excuse my abrupt arrival; no one likes to be surprised coming out of the shower. But it seemed best that we have a little chat, and sooner rather than later. If the robes, hat, and guards did not make it clear, I am Patriarch Shadrach, and I hold the incomparable honor of being Ba'l Melqart's first servant. But only the first, for are we not all in His service? Loyal and loving children, seeking to honor the father and uphold His law? Indeed, is that not the very purpose of the White Isle? Amanuensis, meaning "slave-recorder"?

That being the case, I confess to finding your actions of the last two days troubling.

Your friend does not deserve your venom. True, Gemeti is one of numberless subjects who repay Ba'l Melqart's kindness and protection with loyalty, who place that loyalty, a loyalty not only to a father who guides them but to the city He has built, above petty personal friendships. Can you truly fault her for coming to us with her concerns?

What does it matter if she came to us, or we sent her? We would have known anyway. I can assure you, Gemeti is far from the High Chapel's only source of information.

It seems mastery of one's temper is not numbered among the perfections. Still, you might make an attempt—and I will add, as a brief but perhaps valuable aside, that these two men are members of Ba'l Melqart's life guard, and their staves are primed. And, also, that there are a dozen waiting in the corridor outside whom I did not think to bring into our friendly chat.

All of which is to say, do take your hand off the hilt of that ratchet. Thank you.

Where were we? Yes, my questions. An uncomfortable reversal of your normal position, I know, though one on which I'm going to have to insist.

How did you first hear about Nutesh? We've been aware of his interest in matters better served by the official histories, but in and of itself he seemed no trouble. A harmless sort, at least if you hadn't embroiled him in circumstances so far outside his capacity.

That thing you met in the Shade is another matter. We've known of Sweetness and its mouthpiece for a long time. That sort of knowledge bubbles up here and there, echoes of a time before Ba'l Melqart, before the Spire was built, even. But an inquisitor, despite what the people believe, is not a ratcatcher. One does not go running about imprisoning every blasphemer and apostate, every fool and sinner. One must take a broader view of the city's welfare. We have eyes on Sweetness, and on those who think to visit it.

But still what you've done is a terrible crime, Manet, though I think you have already paid for it. Four fingers left on that pretty hand of yours, and I was told you were the finest harpist White Isle had produced in a generation. Was it worth it? The things of beauty you might have created, the fulfillment you might have felt, the happiness you would have brought to others? What did you trade it for? What do you think to gain?

Truth? And you really mean that, don't you? Or think you do.

Let me ask you something—what do you see, out that window you keep glancing at? You see a very stiff drop, some thirty floors to the street. Beyond that you see the Chapel, and you see the Lower Heights, and the Reach. You see the Isthmus, the great bridges connecting Seaside and Spire. You see a city of endless millions, human and halfling, fettered and free.

And what don't you see? You do not see smoke, and you do not see fire. You do not see these many millions tearing themselves apart in bitter madness. You do not see, or you see very little, murder, rape, theft, brutality. Why do you not see these things?

No, I will not take all the credit, though it is true that we in the High Chapel have our role to play. The reason for the peace which the city has enjoyed this last quarter century—not a perfect peace, because we children of Ba'l Melqart are imperfect creatures, but still—that peace exists because of an idea. A dream, if you will. Or a story, if you will not. Shall I remind you of it, since you seem somehow to have forgotten?

Once upon a time there was a great hero named Kiri, who returned from war to find the city tormented by the tyranny of the Anathema, gone mad with age and power. Ordered to turn his weapons on innocent citizens during the Sanguinary March, Kiri refused, and went underground with Amata, his one true love. After three long years of rebellion, Kiri and his companions fought their way to the Spire, but only Kiri survived the ascent to take his place as Ba'l Melqart and begin the reign of peace and prosperity that we continue to enjoy.

We live in the aftermath of that great tale; we are the happily ever after. What lucky creatures! How blessed!

Suppose—purely as an academic aside, you understand—suppose that story had been tinkered with at the edges. Suppose that story were only eighty percent true, or seventy-five. What would that change? The peace holds true, is it not? Undeniable, unassailable. How exactly that peace came to be, what is that when weighed against the reality of its continued existence?

Honesty is a virtue in small children and house servants. The people do not seek truth, they do not want it, and indeed they do not need it. You could run screaming through the streets telling everyone what you know—or what you think you know, because in fact you have nothing but conjecture and hypothesis, the half-remembered stories of an old drunk, the mutterings of a witch—and it would not change a single mind. During the Jubilee, with their passions at a fever pitch? They would hang you from a lamppost, and they would throw stones at your corpse. I have seen it happen; the cells of the High Chapel have nothing on the cruelty of a mob. And they would be right to do so—for this truth you seek imperils the safety and stability of millions. You think to gamble their prosperity against the interests of your own mad quest? You would put some abstract virtue above their health and safety?

But I'm the fanatic.

In any event, one more question, before we determine what exactly it is that will need to be done with you. The only question, really, one I'm sure you've been tormenting yourself with these last few days.

Who sent you the locket?

(15)

Unknown

7:01 PM

Over here! Over here! No time to ask questions, only to move! That was a fine escape, but they will not take long to follow. Through here and down the alleyway, take your first left and wait in the shadow of the ruined house. I will join you there in a moment.

There is no time to argue, mistress, no time!

~

By the thing that made you, what a leap! A thousand people must have seen your dive, swinging from one awning to the next, and none of them will forget it, though they live a hundred years!

It will all be in vain, unless you listen to me carefully, and do exactly what I say. Go to the back door but do not leave through it, not until you hear the parade passing.

You must move very swiftly then, up into the crowd, and lose yourself among the chanters. They are making their third circuit around the old city, and when they complete it they will gather in the main square to hear the benediction on Amata. You will not go with them—you will head to the bay and find someone to take you seaward.

It is your only chance. High Chapel will be hampered by the crowds, but it will not stop them. They are clever, the High Chapel, they are very clever—but they are not so clever as we are, eh?

Ha! Do not worry, they will never catch me. Of that you can feel certain.

(16)

Utuaa the Ferryman

8:03 PM

Closed for the day. We're closed.

Ten hours I've pulled the line, ten hours today and ten hours yesterday and ten hours every day, all the way back to when I had great broad locks of chestnut and not this shrivel of white. Ten hours is enough, more than enough. You can head north to the Cove; there are crafts that run at all hours. Or there is the bridge, though that would be quite a walk.

Is your house on fire? Your mother dying? A man, then? What else would make a pretty girl so desperate? He must cut a fine line, to put you in such a spin. I tell you something, you mark my words for scripture—let him come to you! What's fought for is cherished above what is given. He ought to be seaside right now, trying to talk some poor ferryman into making one last passage east.

God King willing, he is not successful. Climb in.

Keep your coin. Why do a thing halfway? We will call my strain a sacrifice to Amata, and I would not sully my effort with scrip. A celebration of love, today of all days.

Is he tall? Dark-haired, or fair? Can he dance? It was dance that won me my Mala, though I daresay she liked my shoulders as well. Ten hours a day, it showed then and shows now! But it was my two-step that caught her eye—she didn't suppose a punter could have rhythm. Is he kind, your man? Rhythm is fine, and broad shoulders better, but is he kind? The rest fades, quicker than you might think. You grow used to touching them, and grow used to hearing them talk, but kindness—

~

That's the siren. . . . Very strange, indeed. The last time they rang it there was a blaze in the Lower Heights, took hours to put it out. I'm afraid it'll be a bit longer before you see your young man.

By Ba'l Melqart, he's driven you mad, eh? You'll need to control yourself just the same. The siren means all craft need to divert to the harbormaster or face the High Chapel's wrath. He'll wait a little longer, don't you—

Put it down, girl. Put it down! The waves are high, you might cut me not meaning. Whatever it is they chase you for, a murder will not help.

It won't matter—the cannon follows close after the siren. If we don't turn back, they will blow us right out of the water. A cannon will kill me as surely as a ratchet, and at least I would die honest.

~

They grow closer! We will both be dead soon, if you don't let me signal! What did you do, girl, to have all of the High Chapel after you? It must have been something terrible. Murder? Treason? Blasphemy?

~

Here! Here! The one you're looking for is here, I will have no part of it! I am a righteous soul, by the God King! My soul to his mercy, and my body to the waves!

DAY 3

(17)

Pim, Pav, Pom

5:37 AM

See! See! Not dead! Only wet! Pim told Pav but Pav did not believe Pim!

Liar! It was Pim wished to eat her!

Pav is the liar! Pav is a teller of untruths! Tell him, Pom!

You will drive her back into the water, with all your yelling. Forgive them, mistress.

Forgive us!

Forgive us!

Water, mistress? Sweet water, not skunk water like we prefer.

We would not bring you skunk water.

Though we like it well enough.

Your kind has no taste for water, you will forgive us for saying.

Forgive us!

Forgive us!

Forgive us for saying!

Breed you call Pim. And Pav and Pom.

Or halflings if you are polite.

You are polite, are you not, mistress?

Of course she is! You can see it in her eyes!

A woman of quality.

So halflings it is.

Beachcombers. Kelp farmers.

We stir the dulse.

It must be stirred, or it rots.

It cannot rot. If it rots it is no good for the machines.

If it rots the master beats us.

It must be stirred.

Did you know that the kelp goes into the machines? All of the machines in all of the city, the lights that shine on you in the evenings, and the boats that carry you across skunk water, and everything else also, they are all from the kelp.

It is an important job, to stir the kelp.

You would not have lights, otherwise!

And we stir the kelp, don't we, Pav?

Yes we do, Pim, yes we do!

More water?

We found you on the sand.

Pav found you!

Liar! Pim found you!

Found you together, mistress.

Dark, very dark. Bright lights, strange sounds. Booms also.

Loud booms.

Very loud booms.

We hid.

From the booms.

The booms were very loud.

But they stopped.

They stopped and we went back to stirring.

The kelp needs to be stirred.

The kelp is very important.

And then we found you, mistress.

On the shore, near the kelp pits.

The kelp must be stirred.

Always, always. All the time.

That is what we do.

It is what we are.

It is what we are *and* what we do.

We stir the kelp.

Sometimes we clean the tanks.

A bad job.

There are sharp things in the tanks.

They look like teeth.

They are not teeth, though.

The tanks are not alive, but they are hungry.

No one knows any longer how the tanks work, mistress.

Master says he does but he is lying.

Hush your talk!

Pim does not like it when we talk so of master.

But it is true all the same—you have forgotten how the tanks work, mistress. You once knew, but you do not know anymore.

That is why we have to clean them by paw, because the piece to clean it broke and they do not know how to fix it.

Lies! Lies you tell of master! Foul lies from a foolish half-breed! Master told you! The piece has been sent to the mainland to be fixed! The piece will be fixed!

Pel was lost in the tanks. Caught his tail and could not come back up.

We need to breathe, mistress, like your kind.

Though not as often.

Not as often, but still. Sometimes.

Pel was caught beneath the kelp and he could not breathe.

And that is why he died.

All of us are hes, mistress.

Pim and Pav and Pom and Pel, all hes.

Master says there is a place where they have shes also.

Master says that is where we came from, this place with shes.

You need a he and a she to make more of either, mistress. Did you know that?

Master says that if we never forget to stir, and clean the tanks when they need to be cleaned, then one day we can go to the place where the shes are kept.

It is not true, mistress.

It is true! The things master says are true! You will be jealous when Pim is sent to be with the shes and you are left here!

Pim does not really believe it either.

I believe! I believe! I will work hard, I will stir and stir and not stop stirring, and one day I will go to the place with the shes! Master has promised it! Master has promised it!

Yes, Pim, yes you will.

I will! I will!

Of course you will, Pim, of course.

Pim gets very excited.

It is best not to get Pim too excited.

You ought not lie about master! You ought not lie!

Sorry, Pim.

Sorry.

It is all right. But you ought not lie. It is wrong to lie.

It is wrong to lie.

We must stir now, mistress. You are fine, yes? You have enough sweet water?

Leave her, the kelp needs to be stirred.

If we do not stir, the kelp will rot.

And master will beat us.

That much is true for certain.

(18)

Captain Baldassare

Go away, girl. I'm busy.

Do you see the empty bottle? Am I your first inebriate? A tip, then—we resent superfluous interrogation.

Not me. Someone may have *called* me that, someone may have directed you to me by that title, but it is not mine. Of what would I be a captain? One must have an army to have a rank, and there is only one army in the city, and that army serves the usurper, and I would put my left hand into a thresher before I would wear his colors. Therefore, by process of induction—that is a philosophical term, do not worry if you can't follow it—I am not a captain.

And now that that's settled, be so kind as to find someone else to bother.

Every day, though with particular vehemence on the Jubilee. What can I say? It is a gift. If a bottle is full, I will empty it, though that bottle be filled with the press of grape, or fermented wheat, or my personal favorite, the distillation of potato. You will find it a common enough skill here in the Enclave.

A lovely four walls the usurper allows us, don't you think? On very windy days you cannot smell the reek from the kelp farms, and on very cloudy days the Spire is not visible as a constant reminder of shame. Though windy days generally blow away the clouds, so it is rare to have both at the same time. Still, it's a comfortable retirement, though there are fewer of us every year, the elders dying off, their children forgetting the obligations. The way of the young, eh? To be foolish, to be ungrateful. Is it a kindness he did in allowing us our dotage, in not having purged us after taking the throne? I never made an enemy suffer more than was needed; if we found a man dying we helped him to his end, we did not put him in a cage as evidence of our mercy.

But then, the ways of men are not the ways of gods, are they?

Yes, congratulations, you have caught me in your rhetorical trap. What cunning genius! That much you may have for free, but nothing more. You wish to leaf through the moldy pages of my memory? It is not a lending library; there is a price to pay for my time. A bottle, so I can stand your presence long enough to hold a conversation, and a second bottle that I might forget it rapidly upon its conclusion.

I should have asked for three. But a deal is a deal.

The bottle first, and then we talk.

~

Fine. Yes, I am Baldassare, once captain in the army of the Divine Empress—ha! You cannot even hear it without flinching! A coward, like all the rest. People are such fools, even more foolish than they are feckless. Change the word and the thing itself changes! The Empress becomes the Anathema, and those who bent knee to the first heap curses on the second.

Not for me. The Divine Empress She was, and the Divine Empress She remains. Not that I'm one of those street-corner madmen who hold to the old prophecies; "fleeing and ignorant, unseen and unseeing, blinded by knife and time, She will come among us again." Losers always cling to things like that. But the old days are lost; the age of gold has turned to copper, to pig iron, to shit. We did not deserve Her, and now She is gone, and there is nothing to do but mourn Her death, and our defeat, and the cowardice of those we fought for, and the falseness of our enemies.

And to drink. There's always time for that.

What could I tell you about Kiri that you don't already know? He was the immaculate birth of the ocean and the moon, spoke his first words at twelve hours, spent his childhood strangling snakes and wrestling lions! When his balls dropped a great choir of devas descended from the skies and sang his name in sweet unison! He was so handsome that to look upon him was to go sunblind, and so chaste that he never so much as smelled the sweat of a woman—before he met Amata, of course, Amata, so beautiful. Amata, so kind!

Fine, fine, you bought the bottle. We soldiered together. Came up through the Academy, commissioned the same year, sent off to war together. That God you all pray to? I once saw him whipped by our math professor for coming late to class. I once saw him puke a pint of liquor onto his dress jacket. Once saw him cut through a war-fettered with his ratchet, climb onto his back somehow, tore into its control plate. Saved me and half my platoon.

Hateful bastard.

He was a man like any other. Better than most, worse than most. Trust an old soldier: there is no such thing as destiny. An artillery shell has no name on it, and dysentery kills geniuses as well as fools. But he was too ignorant to know that, and in time the world came to be fooled by his certainty. Not I. An honest man does not rise to the position of street sweeper in this world. Destiny is ambition gilded, so bright and so beautiful it might excuse anything in its service, which is to say, in yours. What kindling did your God use, to see that blaze rise higher?

I wonder.

Three years we spent at the front, and I thought I knew suffering. Cold, hunger, the occasional misfortune of digging a splinter of steel out of your body or of watching your friends die screaming, cradling them as the blood ran from their mouths or their stomachs or the stumps where their legs had been, as they gasped their last and shat themselves. But we have already established, have we not, that I am a very great fool? I had not been home a week when I discovered the truth of the matter—it was the students who were the real victims! Yes, the students, the men dressed like women, long-haired and vague-eyed, and the women dressed like men, shorn heads and constant scowls, and all smoking puff in the alleyways.

And what were their complaints, exactly? They were not allowed to drink and cavort in the streets past a certain hour! They were required to maintain their allegiance to the Goddess who protected and sheltered them! What abuse! What oppression! How right they were to rant of tyranny and call for revolution!

That year before the rebellion was the worst of my life.

No, it was better than what came after. Still, it was terrible. Nothing to do but sit in garrison while the city rotted, watching the things you fought for, the things your friends died for, get pissed on by callow youths and gutter demagogues. Kiri and I would run into each other in the cabarets and dance halls. There was a crooner he used to go with for a while ... En ... Enheduana, something like that. We would drink and talk in great rounding circles, conversations like waves tumbling that never quite managed to go anywhere but left you exhausted just the same. He was like a man who had lost something, or was lost himself, waiting, desperate for a door to open that he could sprint through.

If you have questions about the March, you'd best ask someone else; I can't remember. I am an old drunk, has that not yet become clear? When I wake in the morning my hands shake so badly I cannot hold a toothbrush. I will say this—whatever happened during the Sanguinary March, whatever officers were there, whoever fired their weapons and whomever they fired them upon—they were right to do so. What is a soldier who does not follow orders?

You came from the kelp tanks, didn't you? I can smell the brine. Fascinating creatures, the halflings. Who made them? Not your God King. Not my Empress. And who came before her? Is there anyone still alive who can remember, some sad ancient gumming their teeth and re-calling things forbidden so long ago as to be forgotten? The city dwindles daily, a broken wagon careening down-hill. Let us hope we do not hit a rock, and the craft shatter into a million pieces! Or at least, you can hope that. I pray for it every day.

Anyway, back to the breeds. The men who lived along the shores used to chase them down with dogs, but they have grown so rare that the High Chapel put a stop to it. Foul things, aren't they? Just enough of the human to make them hateful—the grasping hands, the clever eyes—and then what is not human—the gills and their too-long arms, the webbing between their fingers—makes them seem twice as blasphemous. But that is not why we hate them. Shall I enlighten you?

Envy, pure and simple. Every breed has a purpose. It exists to fill a single, certain need. No doubts, no questions. Only duty, clear and clean as noonlight, or the ring of a bell.

Go away now, you have wasted enough of my time. I don't care what I told you and I don't care what you hoped to hear. I care less about the bottle now that it is gone. I care everything for a full one and nothing for one emptied, as is the case with every other man, woman, child, and breed in our sad and miserable city. Anyway, it would not be wise for you to tarry, Amanuensis; the Enclave is as ridden with spies as any other quarter of the city.

Oh, yes, so very subtle. You think covering up your brand is all it would take to disappear without a trace? Who else would be picking at the old wounds of an old soldier? Such a long interview, and the questions so careful, and you without pen or paper! Are you so stupid as to think everyone you meet so stupid?

Manet the Amanuensis, the most exciting thing to happen to the city in a fortnight! They say you've gone mad, that you murdered an old man and were killed in a ferry while trying to escape the God King's justice. You need not fear my tongue, though there are few others of whom you can say the same. See now how quickly the city turns on you? A word from on high and you are mad, a danger. Another word and you may be a bird, or a turtle, or a lost bit of string. Why do you suppose that each new God purges all the books of the last age? There is no such thing as truth, there is only *belief*, and belief is power. You would do well to remember that.

Or don't, it's no matter to me. I have a second bottle to finish.

(19)

Sin-Nasir

11:57 AM

Come in, mistress, come in. Sin's Seaside Bar and Cabaret is open all day during the Jubilee. We're running a special: one kel and you can drink as long as you'd like from the tap without pausing. Coughing counts as a pause. Also vomiting, obviously.

You want to see the queen? She has a room on the top floor. Yes, still dozing. Not everyone is so industrious as you and I.

That's a lovely shawl. Bit warm for it, though.

Certain you won't have a drink?

Perhaps on the way down.

(20)

Enheduana

12:02 PM

Go away, Aya, it's too early.

~

Go away! Come back when the sun is gone, or less cruel at least.

~

Enough, girl, enough! I'm coming.

~

You aren't Aya. Come in anyway; I'll never get back to sleep. You can move the clothes off the chair while I grab the girl. Here she is. Fetch my morning tray—and some tea for my sister from the White Isle.

What, you think I can't tell one of my own? Forty-eight seconds have passed since you knocked, thirteen since you entered the room, forty-nine and fourteen, fifty and fifteen, I can watch you tick them off as perfect as a water clock. How far did you make it? The fourth perfection? Surely not the fifth. Don't be shy, girl, it doesn't matter any longer; one day you'll realize we're the lucky ones.

Anyway, it's obvious why you sought me out. I can see the act already—two trainees of the White Isle, performing together! What sublime harmonies we could make, what fabulous counterpoint! Shame about your finger, but even still we can write our ticket anywhere in Seaside. I'd get top billing, but that's only to be expected, you being a newcomer to the stage, and . . .

I . . . see. A full graduate, then. Excuse me, Amanuensis, for not recognizing you immediately.

~

Foolish girl, I've been waiting for hours! Leave it on the table. I hope you haven't forgotten the matches? Something, at least.

You'll have to excuse me, I've been trying to train her, but . . . well, you can polish tin all you want, it won't become silver. Just a moment now, allow me a morning puff. Helps with the headaches. Too many years in front of the lights gave me trouble with my eyes.

~

Did he send you? Have you seen him? No? I had thought perhaps . . . at least someone has finally come by to learn the truth of the matter. After all these long years of being forgotten, left out of the story as if I never was, as if I'd never been!

Are you comfortable? There's much to tell. Where should I start, even?

I left the White Isle in the summer of my seventeenth year. The third perfection was as far as I could go. The tabla and the reed pipe came as naturally to me as breathing, but when I set my fingers to the long harp, it was like the strings held some grudge against me. A few weeks of failure and the matron called me into her office and . . .

Anyway, three perfections proved more than enough to make me the star attraction in every nightclub in the city, from the Silver Terrace to the Old Town. I wasn't here six months before my name was on the lips of everyone who knew anything, and my tickets were impossible to acquire, even were you the Divine Empr—the Anathema herself. I had a three-week stand at the Imperial and every night was packed; there were men sneaking through the windows and banging at the door of my dressing room. They would demand encores for hours after the show ended. If it had been up to them I'd be singing till dawn, till noon, till I dropped! This was the old Imperial, not the blasphemy which replaced it, a hideous space, terribly vulgar. But then, that's the way of the world these days, isn't it?

I was getting to him—what is the point of perfect memory if you don't allow a person to speak? And now my pipe has gone out. Fetch me the candle on the . . . yes, that one.

~

That's better.

Kiri. Kiri, Kiri, Kiri. He was one of many that came courting, and not the highest. There was a merchant prince from the Old Town who used to promise me mansions, fortunes, paradise. A general, a high-ranking hierophant, for of course what the High Chapel says is not what the High Chapel does. Kiri was not the wealthiest, not the prettiest.

I'm just being honest. The truth, isn't that what you want?

We met at one of the theaters in the Old Town—long

shuttered. I cannot remember who introduced us, or where. I met so many people, as I said; I was the shining light of the season. That season and several before it, and many more after, and even now my star is far from dimmed. But back then I could fill any hall in the city, have them standing in the cloakrooms to catch a note.

It was Gina, at the Blue Door—why, look at that, I did remember. The long harp may have eluded me, but perhaps I have a bit of the last perfection after all.

At first glance he could have been any of the young soldiers returned from war, any of the ones come back healthy, I mean. His uniform was tight around his arms, and he had that way of standing as if he was expecting an injury but would withstand it when it came, made you want to bring him to your chest. We are all mothers, when it comes down to it. And men are all children. Later I heard he had medals, and stories to go with them, but he never told me any. Either they wouldn't talk about the war or it was all they ever talked about, there was no in between. Kiri didn't want to talk about it.

He wanted to talk about everything else, though. Why was the Grand Bazaar where the Grand Bazaar was, instead of closer to the center of the city? And how did the breeds come to be, and what should we do with them? And if the stories about the External were true, that they had no time or lived outside of time, and how could a thing live outside of time? And why were there people starving in Seaside and even near the Spire, and whether the Anathema knew about it, and if so why didn't she do anything, and if not, why not? And whether this new painter everyone spoke of was worth the trip to the Lower Heights, whether any painter was worth a trip to the Lower Heights, if there was any point to painting at all, if there was any point to anything if there was no point to painting. It was like watching someone stoke a fire, heat and light pouring out of him, this great, mad yearning. For what, I can't say. He couldn't either. For me? Sometimes. For the city? I suppose. For himself? But that's only natural; who else is there?

We all burned very bright back then. The city was not like it is now, wretched and drab, gray all the time, gray even when it doesn't rain. The tenements had not yet overrun the Old Town, and there was nothing on Seaside, or barely anything. On warm days we would take a yacht out from the docks and moor on some abandoned beach, just he and I and the waves and the sun. Have you ever made love on a beach? It's not as romantic as it sounds; the sand gets everywhere, even if you lay down a blanket. Still, you should try it. Everyone should try it. Everyone should try everything, while they have the chance.

~

The troubles, you mean? We did not yet call it the rebellion, not until it succeeded. At first I barely noticed. There were riots in the slums, but bad things were always happening in the slums—they were the slums—and anyway I was never in them. It gave a little flavor to the day, a dash of spice. There was not an idle cathouse in the city during the troubles, not an empty seat in a cabaret. In truth I barely thought of it, but it wore on Kiri and the other soldiers. They worried what would happen if the army was called in to establish order. He drank more, with a sort of purpose, as if to poison some part of him, or . . .

I don't know. There are things you never know about a person, however close you grow.

And then came the March. The blood in the streets, hierophants marching down the avenues with their war staves, everyone frightened, skittering from room to room as if the ceiling might cave. For months they shuttered all the bars and cabarets in Old Town. I was reduced to working in a wreck of a place in the Lower Reaches. Rumors all the time, of the rising resistance, of civil war, his name on every one's lips, his name and . . .

I have one for you, Amanuensis—did you ever try that fib about how we could detect lies? You have! What student of the White Isle has not? If they are fool enough to grasp the snake they are well-bitten. And it always works, doesn't it? Do you know why?

Because they are all lying. You make your face serious, and your eyes cold, and you tell them that you know what they are up to, and then you wait while they sputter and admit finally that yes, three months earlier when they said they were out with their cousin they had actually gone up the Scarlet Way, but they feel terrible about it and have been ashamed since, and you nod severely, all the while having no memory of the evening whatsoever, and not caring at all about how they spent it, or with whom.

Do not say her name! I will not hear it; call her something else if you must use her name, as they call the Divine Empress the Anathema. Call her slut, whore, call her spindly-legged and flat-chested, but do not say her name, not in front of me. The things I've suffered on account of that . . . that . . .

He never loved her. I know he never loved her. It was duty, only duty, and Kiri too noble to escape it. But still, to see them etched in effigy, to hear hymns sung to her in the streets! To be forgotten, I who held his head against my chest while he wept, who caught his words with my lips.

At least I can do the same, forget or puff it away. But you don't have the luxury, do you? How long do you think it will be before you cannot control them? The memories, that is. My high C is a touch off, and I had no gift for the strings, but at least my hand does not tremble on my pipe, and I never struggle to remember if now is *now*, or if it is last week, or last month, or twenty years ago. They don't mention that part do they, or they do when we're too young to understand. What is forty and five when you are eight? How could you go back to your family, even if you could find them? Admit your failure, that you were too cowardly to go forward?

What a terrible thing it must be, never to forget. You don't realize it yet because you haven't lost anything, or anything that matters. But you will, that alone is a certainty. What torment, to recall perfectly the line of your breasts once they have come to wither, the musk of every lost lover. Your first sip of wine, the roar of your first crowd, the laugh of a dead friend. The way the sun hit the beach that day, when he came out of the waves shaking his hair and smiling, you and he and nothing else, wanting everything to end in that second, the world snapped shut like an old purse.

They have cursed you, girl. They have ruined you.

Aya! Another pipe; this one has come to its end.

(21)

Sin-Nasir

12:29 PM

She returns! Half an hour with the queen, surely a record.
I tip my hat to you.

Don't mind Ibbi, he's just here to help with the kegs.
Care for a pull? Take a glass of grape at least, God King
knows you deserve it. To face that old hag before she's
even had her first pipe . . .

Yes, we're honored here at the cabaret to be in the
presence of near-royalty. Near-divinity? What do they
call it when you used to fuck God? No doubt there's a
word for it but alas, I lack proper education.

Who knows, it might be true. *Someone* must have
sucked Kiri's cock before the blessed Amata had the
honor, why not Enheduana? And they say she was a great
beauty back in her day, enough to drive a man mad. But
then again, people say all sorts of things, don't they? And
who would be so fool as to believe all of them? It comes

down to the things you have *heard* and the things that you *know*.

Take Ibbi, with those scars on his face, and his thick fists. I have heard stories about how he gained those scars, and what those fists can do. But are they true? How could I know, unless I'd seen it? Perhaps Ibbi feeds orphans and pets stray kittens in his off hours. Just because a beggar by the Seawall will tell you that Ibbi blinded him after a dice game, not with a knife, but with those sausage fingers of his—well, who would believe the word of some old vagrant? Probably a drunk; most of them are.

Though you can't deny it has a certain appeal. A dark alley, a crowd of hard-looking men, the rattle of dice, a quick scuffle, Ibbi's hands spreading wide. The screaming. It's a good story. It meets our expectations, satisfies that morbid tickle. And he certainly looks the part, doesn't he? Sorry, Ibbi. We need things to talk about, and we do not care if those things are true so long as they are entertaining.

Anyway, truth is overrated. What if she is lying, the queen upstairs? What if she never knew Kiri, or knew him only for a night, as she has known so many others? What good would it do to remind her? Knock the pipe out of her hand, tear away her last shred of illusion? We water our liquor down for a reason.

Still, you wouldn't believe the rumors that fly about

this city. Why, just today in the market there was the maddest story going around, about some Amanuensis who started a riot in the old city. First they said they killed her, a few shots from the harbor cannon—that much at least is not fiction; those blasts are loud enough to rattle the damn walls! But then this morning they said that they couldn't find her body, that she might still be alive, and that there was a reward for anyone who helped capture her.

Yes, Ibbi, I heard the same thing. Manet was the name. Long hair, slender form, the small finger on her left hand missing. They say she went mad and killed a man with a ratchet—an old-fashioned model, like the one that you touch at your hip. But that cannot be you, can it? I can see in your eyes that you are no killer. That is not something that I have heard, that is something that I *know*, as certain as the wood beneath my feet, as certain as the sea salt in the air. Now, be a good little girl and not a foolish one, and do not—

(22)

Pirhum

Come in quickly, before anyone sees you. Take a seat in the kitchen, I'll grab my kit. . . .

~

Don't move.

Speaking is moving, Manet.

By the God King, your eye . . .

I take it you will not come with me to the hospital? I can bandage you up, but without a specialist I do not think you will ever see out of it again.

Please?

No, of course you won't. Drink this.

Because it will make what I'm about to do somewhat less painful.

Bite onto the strap.

4:19 PM

Good afternoon.

I thought it was best to let you sleep. Strange to see you back in that bed, even if it has only been a few days. Quite a lot has happened to you in the interim, at least if the touts are to be believed. It is a strange thing, to have bedded a spree killer. They've started to look at me rather differently at work.

The hierophants were here this morning. I don't suppose they'll come back, but that's no reason to push our luck. Have a cup of coffee and go.

~

Congratulations, then. You have unraveled the mystery of your parentage. All it cost was your left eye, a finger, your position, the lives of several bystanders—I suppose they must have killed that old collector? And wasn't there some mention of a ferryman? Collateral damage, I believe they call that. Any others? Just those? Just those so far?

I hope it was worth it. Though she is still dead, yes? Rose or Amata or whatever you call her? Dead and so she cannot hold you in her arms. Dead and so she cannot see what you have made of yourself, whatever that is. Why do you suppose she put you up for entrance to the White Isles? Was it not out of fear for your safety? Was it not to avoid this exact situation, this doom which you have brought about with your ... pigheadedness! So, again I congratulate you. You may add your mother to your list of victims.

Wait! Don't go. I didn't mean that. I've been going out of my mind, Manet. Since you walked out the door two weeks ago I haven't slept more than a few minutes a night. I can barely stomach food; if I had any taste for liquor I would drown myself in it. And then, when the hierophants came by—can you imagine what that felt like? Thinking you were dead? Thinking I'd lost you for good?

I love you. I know you know that. I loved you from the first time I saw you, stopping into that bar after work. Twelve hours I'd been on; there was an accident in one of the factories and they kept bringing bodies in one after another. Tamzi made me come, *just one drink,* he said. I thought I might pass out on the bar but I knew I couldn't sleep yet, the memory of the dead and the ones I had saved, too tired to feel anything but satisfied. Tamzi ran off with ... Gemeti, I think. Was it Gemeti? You could tell me, I suppose. Looking up over my cup and seeing you across the bar, with your dark hair and your eyes that promised everything.

I think you have to choose to love. To push yourself

a bit, like when we jumped off the Seawall as children, staring down at the blue water, forcing our feet over the ledge. Those first weeks together, up all night, talking and fucking, seamless between the two, sharing everything. At least I was. I took you with me everywhere, down every street, into every conversation. I could smell you on me at the hospital, through the disinfectant. I smiled at everyone, every passerby, every vagrant, every patient, the walking wounded and the nearly dead.

Of course you remember, but *what* do you remember, really? Images? Sounds? Sensations? Do you remember those nights in my bed, not just what happened but what you felt? Not just your hand against my chest, or the numbered beats of my heart, but how you felt feeling that? What do you think that was, Manet? Do you think everyone is so lucky as to have known it?

We can go, Manet. We can flee. I've got money, there are other cities . . . we can disappear. Better that than disappeared into the High Chapel or torn apart by the mob. Better than whatever mad quest you've set yourself.

The truth! A sick joke! You lie with every breath. You sound like the penitents outside of the High Chapel, mouthing virtues till they've grown incomprehensible. What will the truth do for you that I can't?

You never loved me, not like I did you. Is it some part

of your training? Always keeping a step back, remembering rather than experiencing? Or is that just you?

Goodbye, Manet. Don't come back. Please, don't come back.

(23)

Rihat

Enter swiftly, mistress, do not dally in the vestibule. The Embassy is inviolate, but that doesn't mean that it's unwatched.

~

Better. You may speak freely in here; there are none who could set ears on the Guests, not the High Chapel nor Ba'l Melqart himself.

You need not worry about me, I can assure you. We caretakers owe our first and last loyalties to the Guests. Do you know how one of our order is chosen? A note arrives on the doorstep one morning, black script on red vellum. It contains a warning of something terrible to come, soon, the next few hours, a day at the most. An accident, or a vendetta, some preventable misfortune. It suggests that rather than await that fate we present our-selves at the gates of the Embassy. Those who do so are taken in and taught the skills and methods needed to converse with the Guests and to serve what needs they cannot satisfy themselves.

Those that do not ... well, the Guests are not wrong. No, not ever.

I was made aware of your impending arrival earlier this morning. One of the advantages of my posi-tion—the Guests keep us supplied with foreknowl-edge. Though it is rare that we are offered anything more than a few hours ahead of our own time. For our own good, no doubt.

An honorific, one that is preferred over External—preferred by we who are their servants. I do not imagine that our masters care.

Ready? Just as well. The Guests pay no notice of time, but for us the clock ticks forward. And there are things you need to know before you attempt the trap.

Have no fear, you are not the quarry. It's an inaccurate designation as the Guests enter into it freely. *Bridge* would be a better word, but that is not what it was called when I first came here and so that is not what we call it now. The trap narrows them, binds them into a shape with which we can converse—in a fashion, at least. They have no words, and discourse only in—images? Memories? You will understand in a few moments, as much as it can be understood. You may ask them whatever you wish—though I would counsel you to think hard before you go inside and not to ask more than you are sure you need to know. Every moment you spend in the trap is one in which you risk becoming... unmoored. I have seen many come out of the trap unable to speak, or walk, made motionless by the knowledge that has been given them. There are chambers in the back for them, though they do not stay long. They forget to eat, and it is not our custom to force food upon them.

I am obliged by the standards of the order to make this risk clear to any who seek our services. You acknowledge that I have done so? Thank you.

There is another reason I would caution you to be swift, and wise—not part of our protocol, only a personal concern. It is not good to know too much of the future. There are questions which are better left unanswered. The Guests know this, which is why they did not indicate that you would arrive this afternoon before earlier this morning, and why they tell me nothing about my own future—though in fairness there must not be much to tell. I have been a brother for forty years and will die one, and likely soon, if my recent cough is any indication. Still, our limitations are... they are blessings, and we are not equipped to exist without them.

Now then. I do not think there is anything else I have to mention. I take it you still wish to go forward? No, they did not tell me. I can read it in your eyes.

(24)

???

???

An open chair beside a roaring fire on a stormy night in the White Isle/a wave from a friend across the marketplace.

A furrowed brow/an upraised hand/a child cocks their head at the feet of an elder.

A circle closes.

A seed sprouts into a flower/a flower casts its bloom/a flower wilts dries dies/a seed sprouts into a flower.

A tower climbs the sky/the gardens bloom red with fire/the gardens bloom red with blood.

A child in a basket/bread upon the water/salt water like the mother's tears.

A girl grows/rots/grows/a city grows/rots/grows.

A bird takes flight/a tram pulls out of the station/a boat sets free of its moorings.

A great feast on an overburdened table/a full glass/a

heavy stomach/a sore head/the dull slow taste of passing days.

A package on a table/a cage unlocks/a wick lights blackens chars spreads.

A drunkard's bottle/the name of a lover/the name of another/the name of one never loved. A compass bearing/a fog light/a load bearing down, down, down.

A mutt in a blind alley sniffs snarls snaps/brume hangs heavy off the Isthmus/open the binding and the book bugs flee fat from their feast.

A spool of thread unravels unravels unravels/a wound picked open/sparks land on dry brush, cosseted by bleak wind.

A tower climbs the sky/the gardens bloom red with fire/the gardens bloom red with blood.

A circle closes.

(25)

Spireside Tram

7:15 PM

Will he be there, Daddy? Will I get to see him?

He's *very busy,* honey, but don't worry, the God King sees all of us—

A cunt, but he's a clever one.

What clever, he's got half the Reach to back his play.

Clever is as clever does—

You bad, girl.

That's what I told him, but he didn't want to listen.

Do they ever?—

Next stop Grand Bazaar, terminating at High Chapel—

Almost there! Almost there!

Yes, pet.

Look Daddy, you can see the Spire!

Make sure to hold my hand when we get there, and don't run off—

Talks like he's every man's friend, but he'd cut your throat soon as look at you.

If you could get him to look at you. Bastard is so high up his own ass he's forgotten we exist.

Maybe it's time to make him remember—

Forget about him, baby, he's not worth the time.

He dresses like he's auditioning as a pimp. Did you see his hat?

And the cravat, don't forget the cravat.

Who could forget the cravat? Like he puked himself and didn't wash it off—

Can I get some fry bread when we get there?

Of course you can, baby.

Excuse me, do you have a coin for an old veteran, down on his—

He's never going to give it to us. We want it, we'll have to take it.

Taking it's the trouble.

Anyone can be up top.

But not everyone is.

Pardon, sirs, could you help an old veteran with a meal?

Fuck off, you smell like piss—

He *was* beautiful, though.

He was gorgeous, baby, but there's no point thinking on that.

It could have gone different. Why didn't it?

Excuse me, young ladies, could you spare a coin for a veteran, down on his luck?

You too sweet. Have a kel.

Give him a mina, baby, no one's got manners anymore—

High Chapel, last stop—

We're here! We're here—

We'll do it tonight, after the Jubilee, when everybody's too drunk to—

Why didn't it go different?

I dunno, darling. I just don't know.

(26)

Imperial Gardens

7:59 PM

Watch where you step, that tree is rotted and will not support you.

There is no need for your blade. Not for us, though we cannot promise the same for those who wait. You may keep it, if it makes you feel better. It would do you no good if we marked you as an enemy. If we marked you as an enemy you would never have crossed below the boughs. Our shafts are sure. Our shafts are certain.

But you are friend and need fear nothing. We will escort you.

To the Spire, of course—where else would you be going?

Few are allowed into our preserve, as is proper, and so stories grow large about us. We are the Gardens, nothing more. We defend the One Above from any who would seek to do them harm. How long? How to speak of distance without a waypoint? Since the beginning, since there was nothing but the Spire, when the Garden grew forever around it, or farther than any of us had ever seen.

No, I am not that old, or not exactly. Your mother—you remember her touch? How her hand felt on your arm, how her voice sounded in your ear? But you do not remember what the hand felt, or the way you smiled when she spoke. We are what we are and what our root was also. I remember what I felt as a sprout, and I remember how Father felt when he uncurled from the bloom, and what Grandfather felt when he saw Father uncurl. If I thought long and hard I could remember the one before Grandfather, remember what he remembered, the days he numbered above the ground, the touch of the wind in those days. And if I thought longer and harder I could remember the one who came before the one who came before Grandfather, and the one who came before the one who came before the one who came before Grandfather, and in time the rain would fall on me and the sun would strike against my branches and my feet would become roots. There are some who have done this, in the high orchards—lost themselves in memory, or chosen to forget.

Yes, I remember that. That is easy—that was in my father's time. Shall I tell you of it as we walk?

We watched and waited in the boughs, high in the

boughs where the humans cannot go. Black-clad they scurried, thinking to hide, but who can hide from the tree in its own roots? There was no hurry. We would wait for them to go deeper, to grow lost beneath the boughs. Then we would strike.

A terrible heat, the bitter-bleak of drawn sap. The first wave a feint to draw our attention, and the quarry reversed, squads of death-sworn soldiers come to the Gardens like borers or bark-beetles, like termites. The night sizzles, great streaks of light scalding the air. One turns with the empty eye of his weapon, our shaft escaping in the moment before it brightens, the scream of the enemy, the shaft red, the enemy silent.

Not all are so fortunate. The root from which we were cut chars, ashes, arms and trunk burned to cinder. A branch of the same tree falls, two men with blades converging, their sharp edges hewing. But we *are* the Gardens, and this *is* the Gardens, and they have come only to die. Their husks are weak, punctured like anther or sepal, and their lights are too bright and terrible but scatter pointless through the trees, while our shafts are always certain. One screams, breaks, trips on gnarled root and thorn-pricked goes silent. One walks listless in small circles, weapon dropped, throat skewered, chest filling with blood. Each acts for each, and not in unity, as we act. It will not last much longer.

Then a sound so loud that there is nothing left to hear, a light from the Spire that makes night noon. Our bows wither, our strings split. We kneel to the One Above.

Such was what my father felt, the last time there were intruders in the Garden.

We failed, as we have sometimes failed. I suppose—I do not wish to remember, it is dangerous—but I suppose we must have failed in the past as well, yes? The One Above was not always the One Above. And there must have been someone before that. How long does the line go?

I cannot say.

Here we leave you; the Gardens go no farther. The door to the Spire is just down this path. The men who await you are friends, and we allowed them passage. But I do not think they are your friends, and you might do well to unfurl your weapon which you have sheathed.

We serve the One Above. His enemies are ours, since the first seed and the first flower. That is our purpose, that is our sole and overriding and eternal end. Who He has marked, we fight as fiercely and as long as we are able.

Isn't it obvious? He has not ordered us to do so.

(27)

High Inquisitor Shadrach

8:19 PM

By the God King, what a troublesome thing you've made yourself. And all for what? For what? Will you do a better job than Him? Will you make the city a paradise? Will you change the taste of tea?

Leave it. I know a mortal wound when I see it bleeding out my chest. No, I don't want any water, it will only make it worse. Nabu, the one with the beamer, is he... damn, but you're sly with that ratchet. I should have brought more men. No, it wouldn't have mattered. The city was slow to realize, but I could tell. Something is ending. Something beginning.

Well, the Spire awaits, you need only climb it. Don't worry girl, it's not locked. If He wanted you out, He would have kept you out, but He did not.

Why? Do you think I have any idea what... no, I wouldn't want to spoil the surprise. You'll find out soon enough. Or you'll be killed during the Ascent, or you'll go rat-shit mad.

More questions? Still? You cannot help it, can you? My life's blood isn't enough, you want answers as well. Sit beside me a moment, I'll tell you what you ask. I don't want to be alone, or only at the very last.

I know as little as you, less probably, just the stories they tell, the stories we share. There were men who held the rank before me, but they did not pass on their secrets. That is not the point of men like me—we do not exist to remember the things that our masters do, we exist to make sure they're forgotten. I've only been Patriarch for seven years. When Kiri climbed this tower I was still a child, running errands for gamblers and rolling drunks for coin.

Lower Heights, born and raised. My mother took in washing and my father died young and handsome. Today the Heights are filled with budding industrialists and second-rate poets, but when I lived there it was only folk who had nowhere else to go, choked tenements and men sleeping beneath bridges. Every block had its clique and its passwords, its sacred oaths and fighting colors. Balassi and I started one with the other boys, sold puff and scuffled with our near neighbors, chains and knives, a cheap ratchet if you were lucky. Who knows how long that would have continued, if I hadn't been done for passing counterfeit kel and sent to reformatory, to be pestered by priests and learn the worship of the God King? I might run half the crime in the city, by now. Or be long dead in a gutter, like my father.

It doesn't fit neatly, does it? But then, nothing is so neat as you'd like; there are always protrusions, excrescences. My first year as an inquisitor, I investigated a string of disappearances around the Grand Bazaar: modestly endowed widows, small merchants come to the city to trade. An innkeeper was poisoning them and burying their bodies in his coal cellar. I figured that out practically by looking at him: a rat-faced man who squealed at the first feel of his restraints. Terrible and tedious, the usual common atrocity, except that I could not find what he had done with the money. He had no safe, and was not the sort to trust a counting house. He had no reputation for gambling, nor for whores. I spent weeks trying to track down his secret, just to satisfy my pride. Would you like to know what he had managed with his ill-gotten gains? To what ends he put his blood money?

He donated it to the orphanage that raised him, every mina and kel. They put his picture on the wall, smiling brightly. We never learned how many men he had killed, how many women, travelers and tourists, a cook who asked too many questions. And yet they still have that picture, a smiling child, bright-eyed and kindly, with a happy future ahead of him.

You will need someone to edit out the extraneous, to give your story its proper buff. When you rise—if you rise—you will find a man who is not yet me and you will make him into me. Remember that. I am a *necessity,* girl. I am more an institution than the God King himself. Or Queen, as it might be soon enough.

No, you only want the truth! I had forgotten. Surely, none of this had anything to do with self-interest. Nothing of ego, of the need to be right, to be special, to be better than everyone else? That the truth might come with power is only a happy coincidence, eh? You will be more likely to find happiness at the top of that tower than you will truth, believe me on that score. A dying man's promise. Truth, and you think you will get it from him!

Sad girl! Foolish girl. You could have been something different. I could have been something different. I had such hopes, once. I believed! You may laugh at me now, but I believed. No, I don't want water, I told you, it would only slow things down. Why prolong it? To bleed a little longer, to feel more pain, to remember? At dusk in the Heights the whole world would light up and we would go wandering, Balassi and I, ignoring our mothers, ignoring the smoke and the smell, ignoring everything, winding through side streets, climbing the bridges, going tiptoe on the rails.

From the top of the rookery you could look up at the Spire, he would, and I would, the Spire which went up forever, which everyone could see, which promised something, whatever that was, to whoever saw it, never saw anything so handsome as Balassi, the muscles in his shirt, his crooked smile, Balassi who is dead now or not, I never had the courage to check, the most beautiful thing I'd ever seen, never seen anything so beautiful, not when I dressed in white and gold, not when potentates and ambassadors begged my blessing... oh, Mother, oh, Mother, what have I done? What did I do? What am I? My soul to the God King, but what if there is no God King?

If you rise, will you watch for me? Will you watch?

(28)

Manet of the White Isles

???

She had dark hair and her dark eyes were wet, and she
held us tightly and then gave us to the woman in white
onto the white boat and behind us the sun reflecting off
the stone quay and the stone walls behind them and the
great stone walls behind that, and alone against it she was
dark, dark. Screaming and weeping and fighting to get
back to her. We would never forget her. We forgot her.

Easy to forget when there was so much to learn. First
was easy, first was one-two, one-two, one-two, one-two,
and who could not manage that? Not all of them, sad little things, stupid little things, trying and trying and one
day crying and next day gone. The second only a little
harder, *this* sound is sharp and *that* sound is flat, as blue
is blue and green is green. And if you can *hear* the sounds
then surely you can *make* the sounds, no secret there, but
they fall away one after another, Ia who walked with us

along the beach, Hillalum too shy to ever speak.

The fourth is hard. No, the fourth is harder but it is not hard. They put the harp in our hands and we set our fingers—we had ten, then—we set them where they told us and then we watched as they watched, hiding smiles, but we could see the traces around their eyes and the edges of their lips. Ninsunu is dismissed soon after, and Tattannu with the very dark hair, we would look at his hair and feel hot in the throat, but he could not figure his fingers and he goes as well.

Four perfections and they take us to the secret spot atop the castle, the spot we all wondered about. White beaches and white castles and inside them the white room, and inside the white room the ones who came before, dressed in white, bound with white rope. For their own good, the teachers assure us. Mouths speaking old words and eyes seeing old things. There is too much in their heads; they cannot take any more.

So? So? Who can be bothered? The people in the room are old, and we are young. As fish to fowl. And there was still so much to learn. Who would think to quit halfway through? To see the looks on the faces of the teachers, to board the black boat which leaves the White Isle and does not return, like that sad old bitch we met.

And still so much to learn, so much to learn. Left foot goes *there*, ankle up, and right foot goes *there*, ankle down, and on the second step the left hand tilts right, and on the third step the right hand tilts left, and how *easy* it all comes, easier than any of the others, fat Uppulu or foolish Zakiti, who needs to be taught everything a dozen times and then a dozen times after that and *still* cannot manage it half so neatly as we can. Left foot *there*, ankle up, and right foot *there*, ankle down. Sit quietly and move the last bend on our last finger, the narrow nubbin of our nose.

The youngest to reach six perfections in all the order's perfect memory, and they mutter of us in the great hall and the side rooms. But six is not seven, is it? No, six is not seven. Alone in the room all white, alone alone alone alone alone but so busy, a million million things happening every moment, the rustle of the wind on the windows the dust in the corners each strand and hair and flake the blood coursing from your heart down into your fingers and toes and the blood coursing back from your fingers and toes into your heart. A million million every instant, and there are a million million instants to each instant. Impossible, not what the brain is for, impossible, cannot be done, impossible, and then one day not only possible but necessary, one day and it cannot be turned off even if you wanted to. Sometimes you want to.

The instructors assembled: what was served for breakfast on the third day of winter two years past? What was candidate Zakiti's final word, the day before she chose the ocean rather than leave White Isle? How many buttons did she have on her coat? How many clouds were in the sky above her, and what shapes did they form? On and on and on and on, but we do not stutter and we do not falter and in the end the brand is a formality, brand or no brand makes no difference. We are the thing they made us.

Stay or go? Go, of course. To do all of that and rot? What is the point of remembering everything when everything is so forgettable? We will return soon enough; the white room is not so far away as we had thought. Until then . . . what? The boat leaves for the city and we stand at the prow and the things we felt then, oh, the things that we felt we can remember but cannot say, would not say if we could, too precious to be spoken or spread.

Arriving and trying to filter the sounds the scents the scents especially, body odor and dog shit and meat cooking in the bazaar, effluvia endless effluvia. Horrifying and then exhilarating, so ripe and so rich, each sensation and picture and thought slotted and collated, our training unconscious and perfect. Ate syllabub and salt fish, burnt ends and fried offal, oyster pulled fresh from the sea, a slice of grapefruit with crystal sugar but did not like the taste, bitter but we cannot forget, never forget. Listened to music in the parlor music on the street corner music in smoky bars music in the concert halls music in a garden none of it as good as we can make but music all the same. Felt muslin felt silk felt ribbon felt samite fox fur peacock feather lamb's skin the corded muscle of man the embonpoint of woman.

How small was the White Isles! A quarter century spent apart from everything!

Pirhum so handsome, but like someone who is not sure of it, blushing and looking down at his feet, blushing and looking back up at us. And later the moon coming through the window and him sticky on us and for a few minutes not thinking about anything only the breeze coming through the window, like death, yes, but a kind death, better even than sleep because there are no dreams to intrude upon the nothing.

Happy for one month and then two and then half pretending and then all pretending and then not pretending anymore, and him wondering what has he done? Just stayed the same, those glasses and that smile, that smile which felt too much like worship. Wanting to poke a bit, ashamed for wanting but wanting all the same, to prod, to wound, to see him scowl, to see his wide eyes go sad.

Are they all like that? Pretending, feigning, forcing on the mask, hoping they will grow to fit it? Or is it us? Just us wanting more? Just us?

Coming home that night a night the same as every night Pirhum's smell hospital disinfectant and sweat beneath that and his cat we hear it in the back room but smell it everywhere and the moonlight filtering through the curtain the same as every night except on the counter is a package in brown paper like they use to wrap loin kidney sweetbread but inside is not loin kidney sweetbread inside is a locket, and inside that locket a woman. Who is the woman? Pirhum laughing, shrugging, growing worried. Who is the woman? Walking down the street in the morning. Who is the woman? Drinking in the afternoon. Who is the woman? The bar is full and they are all laughing, drinking and laughing, who is the woman, all happy, Pirhum and Tauthe and Gemeti and they are all laughing laughing laughing. Who is the woman? In bed with him on top of you, moaning and writhing but who is the woman? Who is the woman? Who is the woman?

One foot in front of the next, right goes *there* and left goes *there*. Near the top. You will manage it. Mother managed. And Father also.

(29)

Ba'l Melqart

Come in, come in. Enter boldly, your troubles are all behind you. Will you take water? Wine? How are you . . . feeling? Everything in order? The passage through the Spire can be quite taxing. When poor Laqip came up he could not stop babbling, and did not remember who he was, or he remembered all of it all at once, which is even worse.

Wait, that isn't right—Laqip didn't survive the ascent. Only I survived. Would you like some wine? Or perhaps some water, after all your struggle?

It is quite a thing, becoming God. A god. Becoming a god. I cannot say it is altogether pleasant. But then, nothing is only one thing or another. And there are some nice parts. They chant your name every day, which is helpful when you forget it. You can look like anything you want, and some days I go swooping over the city as a great black bird. It is a fine thing to fly. I perch on ledges and I watch the people go by. There are so many of them, they are everywhere, old men dying alone in the alleys of Seaside and babes being born in the Reaches, and pretty girls giving themselves to their lovers for the first time and old women remembering when they had done the same, and bugs in their clothing and rats in the alleyway and birds staring at those rats with knowing hunger and a million and a billion other things. And they all pray to me, Manet, they all pray. And how can all their prayers be answered? For the bird prays to catch the rat, and the rat prays to escape the bird, and the boy prays to land himself a girl, and the girl prays that she might always be free.

Would you like some water? Or perhaps something stronger? Wine? I have anything you might want, though I no longer eat or drink. That is the one of the things about becoming God. A god. You do not eat, and you do not drink. You don't miss it, though. You hardly ever think about it. The other thing goes away also. You will miss it for a while, but then you will forget it. You will forget many things, I'm afraid. That's the reason for the White Isle, to serve as memory. Did you know that? No, no one knows the why of things anymore. I am at the head of it, and even I do not know the why. The city is old, the city is *ancient*, the city has been for so long you cannot even begin to imagine. Sometimes atop the Spire you start to think that you are as old as the city, that you were always here.

But you aren't! Or I wasn't. You are proof of that. You look just like her, just like my Amata. Her spitting image. Except that ... Amata had both eyes, did she not? Yes, I am sure she did. One, two, two eyes. You only have one. Don't worry about it. When you sit on the throne you can have as many eyes as you want, you can have eyes running up your arms and your legs and on your back and underneath your hair, though I don't know why you'd want them. Who needs more than two eyes? Aren't two plenty? Who would wish to see more than that?

Well, whatever you want you can have, just tell me first, if you please, if you don't mind. Yes, sit down there—across from me, so I don't miss anything. Take your time, we've all the time in the world. Would you like some water first? Or perhaps wine?

Who I am, of course! How it all happened. From the very beginning, if you please. I have ... it sounds silly, but I have ... there are holes; sometimes I cannot quite recall ... you'll clear all that up for me, won't you?

~

That is ... that is not a kind joke to play on your father. Assuming I am your father. You shall get no wine that way! Nor water, either.

~

Why would I know! What would be the point of you, if I knew? Why would I have set it all in motion, if I knew? If I could remember still? Why did I send you the locket? Why did I clear the field? Was I not there to guide you every step of the way, did I not play the role of your loving father? And so I must be him, mustn't I?

Mustn't I?

But you asked for water, didn't you? Or was it wine? And I said I would get you some but then I forgot to do so. Forgive me! It is taxing, being God. A god. My memory is sometimes . . . but I told you that.

Where were we? Yes, you were just about to tell me everything. Who I am and where I came from, and how I came to become a god. It must be quite a story! Of course, it is the same as the one they tell every year around this time, the same as the one they are chanting in the square at this very moment! But still it would be nice to have someone else tell it. The way they tell it . . . I'm sure it's . . . it must be true, or why would all of them say it? Why would they say it if it were not true?

~

But I don't *know* what I remember! Don't you understand? Are the things I remember the things that happened or are they only the things they say? They say them so often, how could I not start to believe them?

There was the Spire... you came up the Spire? Of course you did. One must to get here. Three of us made it through the Gardens, but only I survived the ascent. Wait... no, your mother survived, didn't she? And poor Laqip, though only part of him. Poor Laqip. No. No, it was only your mother and I. And Laqip, but he was broken and did not count. And it was better to let the city forget him. Yes, that was it. That must have been it. As for your mother... as for Amata... what a beauty she was, I can still remember!

~

Sent men? After Amata? Why would I do a thing like that? Why *would* I do a thing like that? Amata did not survive the ascent. No, of course she did, yes, because Amata was your mother. We wished to keep it secret. Yes, that must have been it. We must have decided that it would be better if she went into hiding, and if she took you with her. Who was she hiding from? Who would there be to hide from, after I took the seat?

And then I forgot about her... I mean, forgot that she

had made the ascent. I could never forget about her.

Never.

You will take it from me, yes? It is the least you can do, if you cannot tell me who I am. If you cannot help me remember, then at least you should make me forget.

Please, daughter. Daughter? Daughter? In any event. There needs to be a god, always one, never more. And since you are at the top of the Spire, it has to be you. You will like it, being a god. You can turn into a bird and fly anywhere you want, and the people below cheer your name, and say such sweet things about you! Who would not start to listen, after a while?

Water? Wine?

Acknowledgments

Some people help out when you're writing your book: my agent, Sam; my editor, Carl; and the other folks at Tordotcom Publishing. Thanks!

Other people just help out with general life stuff: my family, Mom and Dad and David and Alissa and Michael and Marisa and my aunt Connie and my cousin Johnathan, who keeps me in touch with the youth. Grateful for the friends I made as a child, that I can watch them care for their own: Bobby and Heather and Elaine, Michael and Grace and Ida, Peter and Kat (plus Joe, have a drop for me). Grateful for the folk I met in college, once upon a time, John and Co., Alex and the long-suffering Katie, Will and Jess and the young prince. Grateful for the far-flung friends I've made since: Kiki in Tokyo, Myke in Brooklyn, Nazia in London, Andy and Eva outside of it, Lisa and brother Will in Oxford, Rob in Uganda, unless he's gone by now. Grateful for the LA crew: Becca, Rachel, Gui, even though you deserted us, Brian, Casper and Cambrian, Garret, whose life I adopted. Grateful for the SELAH folk and the volunteers and staff on the Suicide Prevention Hotline, 6 shift shout back. Grateful for L.

About the Author

DANIEL POLANSKY was born in 1984 in Baltimore, Maryland. He is the author of the Low Town series, the Hugo finalist *The Builders,* and *A City Dreaming.* He currently resides on a hill in eastern Los Angeles.

TOR·COM

Science fiction. Fantasy. The universe.

And related subjects.

*

More than just a publisher's website, *Tor.com* is a venue for **original fiction, comics,** and **discussion** of the entire field of SF and fantasy, in all media and from all sources. Visit our site today—and join the conversation yourself.